A Cup
of
Kindness

a
pale horse
production

Library of Congress Control Number: 2002116171

ISBN: 0-9710362-1-7

A Cup of Kindness

Relating
The Further Adventures & Noble Deeds
of
Cabal, King Arthur's Dog,
as told
by
Cabal Himself

*   *   *   *

Translated Out of the
Canine Tongue
by
Merlin the Wizard

*   *   *   *

Inscribed by me,
Brother Blaise,
St. Francis' Friary,
Crastor-upon-Sea, Northumberland

part I

" . . . a living dog is better

than a dead lion."

— *Ecclesiastes 9:4*

I   *Let Sleeping Dogs Lie*

Images were forming, blending, dissolving. . . of a reddish-brown dog with his jaws clamped tightly upon the hilt of a gleaming sword . . . of a great throng of Britain's finest nobles kneeling before my master Arthur and calling him their liege lord . . . of a man with the face of a rat taking aim at my master with his deadly crossbow . . . of Arthur's coronation in Westminster Abbey and of Bishop Baldwin placing a crown on my master's head and the mantle of kingship about his shoulders . . . of a royal procession through the streets of London with everyone shouting "Hail Arthur, King of the Britons!"

And then came further images . . . of the sudden and mysterious disappearance of the huge black stone in St. Paul's Square . . . of a great squabble amongst the barons and nobles concerning Arthur's right to be king; some said he was the true-born king of Britain and some said he wasn't and would oppose him to the death . . . of a terrible battle on the seacoast against an army of Saxons, huge blond men who fought with long knives and battleaxes . . . of Lupus and me fighting for our lives against a pair of vicious, rangy mongrels who belonged to the huge blond men . . . of our glorious celebration after we'd won the battle and especially of a heaping platter of venison bones that was my own special reward. Yumm, I was really enjoying the image of that heaping platter of venison bones. They seemed so real I could almost taste them.

"Cabal," a voice whispered softly, "time to wake up, boy, time to get your juices flowing." Someone was rubbing the fur on the back of my neck. I liked it, but I was deep in some lovely dreams involving venison bones and wasn't eager to wake up.

When I finally opened my eyes, everything was dark. Then my little dog brain began to function and I knew that Arthur was beside me, tousling my fur. He was grinning like anything, and I wondered what he was so cheerful about.

Then everything came back to me. It was the wee hours of the night. We were perched on a lonely mountaintop somewhere in the north of Wales. And most important of all, we were just about to do something that I *really didn't want to do.*

"C'mon, old sleepyhead," Arthur said, running his fingers through the fur on my chest. "You've been itching for a little excitement, right? Well, it won't be long now."

Ha, I thought, don't make me laugh. Yes, I *had* been doing a fair amount of itching lately. But not out of any need for excitement. No indeed. Not when King Ryence had about a million guys in his stinking Northgalian army. Not when all we had was fifty valiant fellows and a single pair of stout-hearted dogs.

"C'mon, Cabal," Arthur said, "let's go see how things are looking out there."

Arthur beckoned to Sir Lucan and Sir Griflet, and then the four of us crept up to the top of the ridge. There, spreading out across the plain before us, we saw a multitude of tiny flickering lights. My eyes couldn't tell me what they were but my nose could; they were the campfires and cookfires of King Ryence's army—campfires and cookfires we would soon be seeing much closer up, if we really went ahead with Arthur's insane little plan. Out beyond all those tiny lights we could see the torch-lit walls of the City of Carmelide. That was our goal on this moonless July night, and only one thing stood in our way of getting there—the umpteen million Northgalians who were encamped between us and the city.

After we'd had our fill of the unnerving sight of all those flickering lights, we padded softly back to where the rest of Arthur's men were waiting. Kei and Merlin were there, and so was Lupus, my own rough-and-tumble brother.

In a very soft voice Arthur told them how the land lay. "It's risky, Arthur," Merlin said in response, "but they won't be expecting it. And that's why I feel sure we can bring this little caper off."

Merlin, I said to myself, you darn well *better* feel sure we can bring this little caper off. Because if you're *wrong*, a certain dog and his brother just might end their day being the choicest morsels in the stewpots of some stinking Northgalian soldiers.

No, despite the fact that Merlin had a good bit of confidence in Arthur's plan, I really had my doubts. Deep down inside I felt a strong sense of foreboding; I felt that something very bad was going to happen. No, despite the fact that Merlin is almost always right, the truth of the matter is that he *isn't* always right. I'd once heard old King Uther say you can count on Merlin to be right ninety-nine times out of a hundred. I hoped this wasn't going to be the *one* time out of a hundred when Merlin was *wrong*.

Then it was time to put Arthur's bold little plan into action. Arthur eased himself up onto Tawnyfoot, and soon the others were mounting up also. Kei was on Brutus and Hervey sat high up on a tall bay stallion his father had given him. Merlin was riding a huge black charger named Bryn, a wise old warhorse with whom I'd become quite good friends. When all of the riders were mounted, Lupus and I took up our positions to the side and slightly behind the back legs of our masters' horses. No matter how fast Tawnyfoot and Brutus went, that's where we had to be. If we strayed, we stood a good chance of getting trampled.

Pairs of riders began moving slowly down the steep incline, Sir Lucan and Sir Griflet in the lead. When our entire troop was on level ground, the riders shifted into a different formation. Now they were spread out in a single wide line, except for Sir Lucan and Sir Griflet, who rode side-by-side in front. Arthur, Merlin, Kei, and Hervey were positioned in the center of the long line, and Lupus and I were right behind them, right where we were supposed to be.

Sir Lucan and Sir Griflet stepped up the pace, first to a trot and then to a canter. As we approached the outermost fires of King Ryence's army, fires that were now just glowing coals, the horses broke into a gallop, and Lupus and I had to run like anything to keep up. Our charge took us past a great many men who were startled into wakefulness by the sudden thrumming of horses' hooves. Now we were smack-dab in the middle of that huge Northgalian encampment.

Men began shouting, and soon others were taking up their cries. Believe me, I didn't much like it that there were folks up ahead of us who knew we were coming. Arthur's men rode straight on, not bothering to do any fighting against the fellows who'd begun rushing about like angry ants on an anthill. Right then we had just one thing in mind—getting our furry little backsides through that stinking horde and reaching the safety of Carmelide.

Just when it seemed we were nearly through, a huge mob of Northgalians sprang up in front of us, fellows who were intent upon blocking our path. They were all on foot, not on horseback, but they possessed a gruesome array of swords and spears and pikes. Sir Lucan and Sir Griflet would now execute some fancy maneuver so that we could avoid them, right? *Wrong!*—they just spurred their horses all the harder, intending to bash their way straight through those assembled fellows. Good luck to *us*, I shouted inside my head—we're going to need it.

All this time I'd been sticking to Tawnyfoot's heels like a furry glob of glue. Whenever she zigged I zigged, and whenever she zagged I zagged. But when Tawny made a sudden sideways leap, that's when my troubles began—for I'd already anticipated going in the opposite direction. And right at that moment somebody whacked me a good one high up on my shoulder. I went tumbling head over heels and came down hard on my side. I was up again in a jiffy—just in time to dodge my attacker's follow-up blow. By then Tawny and Arthur had disappeared into the midst of a terrible tangle of men and horses. Now I was on my own. If I was going to make it to the safety of Carmelide, I would have to do it on my own.

What had happened to Lupus? I had no idea. Maybe he'd followed Kei into the middle of that frightful fracas. I certainly *hoped* not. He and I were much better off taking our chances with the Northgalian foot soldiers and their gruesome weapons than in amongst the flying hoofs of those rampaging horses. I dearly love horses, but believe me, they can inflict a large load of hurt upon innocent creatures like Lupus and me.

My plan was to dart off to the left, the one direction in which things seemed fairly quiet, for everyone's attention was focused on the melee I was trying to avoid. But just as I thought I was in the clear, a squinty-eyed Northgalian spotted me.

"Stop, you filthy cur!" he barked out, whirling his long-handled axe right at my head. I fell flat on the ground at the very instant that his razor-sharp blade skimmed across my back. I'd been quick but not quick enough—for that maniac's blade had plowed a neat little furrow right through my fur and all the way down to my naked flesh. The only good thing I can say is that that blasted blighter's blinking blade had *mostly* missed.

With a burning sense of relief I sprinted forward, leaving that odiferous dog-hater in my dust. At last I was free and clear of the whole stinking Northgalian army, with the torch-lit walls of the city just a few hundred yards ahead of me. Off to my right the horrible ruckus I'd been trying to avoid had finally sorted itself out and a group of riders had broken free. Of course it was Arthur's war band, and they were riding like blazes toward the gates of the city.

And just at that moment those lovely, welcoming gates came swinging open. "Very nicely timed, you excellent chappies," I sang out, "very nicely timed indeed!"

As the horses crowded through with a great clattering of hooves, I charged toward those gates with every ounce of speed I could muster; and as I tore through the night, I could feel the cool air stinging the bare patch on my back.

And then a terrible thing began to happen—those lovely, welcoming gates were *closing* again! "Now, wait just a bleeding minute!" I yelped.

The gap between the two huge doors was narrowing fast. What if I didn't *make* it? What if those gnat-brained idiots locked me *out*? In the next moment I hurled myself at the tiny slit that remained. That's when I learned what a tight squeeze really is—for those damnable gates did their level best to squish my poor guts out.

But then I was *through*, and my sense of relief outweighed all my other aches and pains. Arthur spotted me and came rushing over, and old Merlin wasn't far behind him. Both of them looked anxious and relieved at the same time.

They hugged me and petted me and gave me a delightfully warm welcome—exactly the medicine I needed. Unfortunately, I wasn't able to enjoy their warm welcome for very long. For right at that moment we heard Kei's desperate shouts. "*Lupus!*" he bellowed. "Where in blazes is Lupus? *Hasn't anybody seen my dog?*"

II   He's My Brother

We looked frantically for Lupus—searching, shouting, hoping—but all the while I was pretty sure what the truth really was. Lupus wasn't here, and that could only mean that he hadn't made it to the safety of Carmelide. My poor brother was still out there in the dark, still out there among all those filthy, stinking Northgalians. Heaven only knew what they would do to him if they got their grimy paws on him.

Kei, accepting the fact that Lupus wasn't in the city, began shouting for the gatekeepers to get their damnable gates open. "Get 'em *open*," he roared, "get 'em open *now*! I'm going back out to look for Lupus!"

"What's the difficulty here?" A man stepped out from the shadows of the gate-tower. He was a large and imposing fellow who was decked out in a very fancy uniform; by all appearances, he was a person of considerable authority. "Are some of your men still out there?" he asked.

"No," Arthur replied, "our men are all accounted for. But one of our dogs is missing. Some of us are going back to look for him."

"One of your *dogs*, is it? Well, *that's* a relief; not so great a price to pay, considering what you've been through.

If I were you, I'd be thankful it was nothing more than that. After all, it's only a dog."

"Only a *dog!*" shouted Kei, who by this time was shaking with rage at the words of this busybody and the delay he was causing. "Only a *dog?*" he shouted again. "*Yes*, and this is only a *fist!*" Quicker than you could say Joseph of Arimathea, Kei punched that foolish fellow right smack in the face. Blood spurted from his nose, making a royal mess of the fellow's silly uniform; and now the fellow was bent over, coughing and spewing blood down onto the cobblestone pavement. Kei's sturdy little punch had knocked that pompous fool all the way to the middle of next week.

The gate-guards stood there with their mouths hanging open, not quite believing what they'd just seen. And because the fool Kei had punched was in charge of them, those poor blokes didn't know what they should do. But when Kei directed his angry glare at them, it didn't taken 'em long to figure out the best course of action—it was time to get those massive doors open again.

Getting them open again wasn't a simple matter, for those huge doors were a vital element in the city's defenses, and there were all kinds of chains and levers and pulleys that needed attending to. But they were able workers, and they had the added incentive of not wanting Kei to throw any punches in *their* direction.

When the complex mechanisms had been worked and the gates were finally free, the gate-guards shoved them open. A small bunch of us dashed outside to have a look. The torches on the walls cast their light across the dry moat and on out to a second set of defensive ditches; beyond that, everything was dark and shadowy. Off in the distance I could just make out some blurry shapes where the first of the Northgalian soldiers were positioned. As far as Lupus was concerned, I couldn't see anything that looked at all promising.

A terrible feeling of hopelessness crashed down upon me. Finding my brother out there among all those enemy soldiers seemed futile. By then he'd probably been captured or wounded or *worse*. And at that moment I could think of only one thing to do. I lowered my head and prayed for all I was worth.

"Oh Great Maker," I said softly inside my heart, "please look kindly on my brother Lupus. Oh Kind Protector of the fishes, fowls, and four-footed beasts, if it be Your will, please look kindly on my brother Lupus. He's still a young dog, Great Maker; and if You'll pardon me for saying so, he's one of Your finest creations. So please, Kind Protector, grant my brother his properly allotted time. Can three or four years be long enough for a good-hearted fellow like Lupus? If it be your will, Great Maker, please look kindly on my brother Lupus."

When I finished, I glanced up into the eyes of Merlin the Wizard. I knew that he'd been eavesdropping on the innermost thoughts of my heart.

"Cabal," he said, "the Great Maker expects His creatures to do their part, too. Now it's time for you to do *your* part; put those keen senses of yours to work, Cabal. Listen really hard. Listen for anything that sounds like a dog."

I closed my eyes and concentrated. I really did. I listened for all I was worth. And you know what? I didn't hear a blessed thing that sounded like a dog. So much for my vaunted powers of hearing.

But all of a sudden something *did* begin to register on my senses, though not on my sense of hearing. For it was right at that moment that I began to *feel* something, not *hear* something. And what I was feeling was anything but pleasant. My head started to spin and my body began hurting all over; everything seemed horribly confused and jumbled up. What's going on? I wondered. And then I *knew* what was going on. Everything that I was feeling wasn't what *I* was feeling—it was what *Lupus* was feeling! Somehow—but don't ask me how—Lupus' feelings were being transmitted to *me.*

Those feelings were *horrible*—they were the worst feelings I have ever experienced. It was as if my life was slipping away from me; my sense of consciousness grew fainter and fainter and there wasn't a blessed thing I could do about it. And then everything went *blank.* It was as if I didn't exist at all.

Suddenly I was back to being my own self again. Lupus' feelings were no longer being transmitted to me. My word, what a terrifying experience. And what a huge relief when it was over. But what in the world did it mean? What did it mean that I was no longer receiving Lupus' feelings?

18

Before I had a chance to think any more about it, some powerful instinct buried deep down inside me took complete control of me. Before I even knew what I was doing, I went charging straight off into the darkness, making a beeline for the Northgalian soldiers' camp. "Cabal," Arthur shouted after me, "wait!" I could hear Arthur and Kei and Merlin stumbling through the darkness behind me.

Not so long ago I'd been doing everything in my power to *escape* from the Northgalians, and now here I was charging right back into their midst. What the heck was I thinking! But I couldn't help it. Deep down inside me I knew there was still a very slim chance that Lupus was alive; and if he was, I had to do everything I could to help him. Lupus is my brother.

Through the gloom I spotted several men gathered around something on the ground. Two of them reached down and took ahold of it, and now they were lifting it up. And I knew what they were lifting—it was Lupus! Those filthy Northgalians were putting their paws all over my own poor brother. Without waiting for Arthur and Merlin, I went for them, barking and snarling and snapping. "Watch out!" one of them shouted. "Here comes another one!"

It was plain to see they were afraid of me. They dropped what they'd just picked up and snatched at their weapons. But hearing the rapid approach of my companions, they must've figured it was time to get out of there, for in the next moment they disappeared into the darkness.

"Lupus!" Kei shouted. "Is it Lupus?" Yes, it was my poor bedraggled-looking brother. And he was lying frighteningly still.

"Wait!" shouted Merlin. "Don't anybody touch him!" And then he swung his staff in a wide arching circle above Lupus' head, shouting "*Bestia animare, fera resuscitare, canus excitare!*"—or some such words.

Immediately I felt a terrible jolt. A burning sensation began shooting through my body, followed by a great surge of energy that I could feel coursing through every muscle and limb. *Holy Jerusalem*, I thought! Where in the heck did *that* come from?

And then we heard the first of Lupus' whimpers. He blinked his eyes a few times and stared rather blankly at Kei and me. My brother had no idea where he was or what in the world had happened to him. But my own dear brother was *alive*, and his whimpers and moans were music to my ears.

Kei scooped up my brother and held him against his chest, and then we all set off, back toward the torch-lit walls of Carmelide. As we moved into the light, I saw a weary but grateful dog licking weakly at his master's face.

"Merlin," I heard Arthur say softly to his old teacher, "I hope you're going to explain to me what just happened back there."

"I think Lupus was stunned, Arthur; he must've received a major blow to the head. But I think he's going to be fine."

Knowing my master as I do, I was pretty sure Merlin's explanation didn't completely satisfy him, and it certainly didn't satisfy me. But perhaps there isn't any easy way to explain what really did happen back there. Having been around Merlin as much as I have, I know there are quite a lot of things in heaven and earth that aren't easy to understand—especially by the mind of a gentle, grass-eating dog.

By the time we reached the city, a huge crowd of Carmelidians was there to greet us, and leading the welcoming party were King Leodegrance and his daughter Gwinevere. That lovely girl was beaming at Arthur and looking radiantly happy, and Arthur was beaming right back at her. My word, also among our welcomers was Sir Bedivere. How in blazes did *he* get here ahead of us, I wondered? And then I heard the cries of another young welcomer, a young welcomer whose greetings were entirely for me.

"Cabal!" he shouted, "Cabal le Savage! Oh how I've missed you—*you no-good mangy mutt!*"

It was Melleas, Gwinevere's pesky little brother. I guess he hadn't forgotten me from that time in London when we'd shared some crazy adventures. Letting him know I appreciated his warm welcome, I gave it right back to him in the form of a vigorous face-licking. That's when I discovered that somebody'd been breakfasting on strawberry preserves, barley cakes, and soft-boiled eggs!

Yumm, that little taste of Melleas' breakfast made me realize I was starvingly hungry. Truthfully, I was *ravenous*!

Just a few minutes later, every one of us was gulping down a hearty breakfast not unlike what I'd previewed on Melleas' face—hot and buttery barley cakes, soft-boiled eggs, and bread crusts soaked in goat's milk.

My hunger satisfied, I turned my attention to all the discussions around me; and that's when I learned how folks in Carmelide were faring. The city, I learned, was now in its third week of the Northgalian siege—that was the *bad* news. But small boats had been slipping in from the river under the cover of darkness and bringing fresh supplies—that was the *good* news. King Ryence didn't have many boats, so he had a tough time stopping them. In fact, that's how Sir Bedivere reached the city ahead of us, by slipping in from the river under the cover of darkness. He was the one who'd told the gatekeepers to be watching for us in the wee hours of the morning.

Now folks expected King Ryence to do one of two things—either he'd make an all-out attack on the city, or he would pack it in and head for home. The longer he dithered the worse things were for him because he had a huge army to feed and because he knew that Arthur would certainly send help. Now Arthur had—in the form of *us*—though our meager little war band wasn't the powerful army King Ryence had feared might come.

Maybe you're wondering why Arthur had such a small war band. First of all, that's what he preferred. Arthur liked traveling with a small group of handpicked fellows, fellows he knew he could always count on. But an even bigger reason was that every one of Britain's major armies was tied up right then dealing with a variety of urgent matters. King Lot and his army were down in the southeast of Britain trying to contain the large groups of Saxons who'd been overrunning the countryside down there. King Nentres and his army were up on the Scottish border playing cat and mouse with King Angus, the wily leader of the Scots. And King Uriens and his army were in South Wales, trying to chase down several bands of Irish marauders who'd been creating havoc in that region.

That's why it was up to us, and us alone, to provide aid and succor for King Leodegrance. That's why we'd come and why we now found ourselves inside a city being besieged by umpteen million smelly Northgalians—umpteen million smelly Northgalians who intended to do vicious things to every living creature in Carmelide—dogs included.

III   *The Assault on Carmelide*

As the first hints of day appeared in the eastern sky we learned what King Ryence had decided—for that's when the Northgalians attacked. First we heard shouts from the guard towers and then we heard clarions resounding all across the city. Cries of "To arms! To arms!" reverberated around us as the defenders of the city dashed to their pre-arranged battle stations. Arthur's men snatched up their weapons and rushed to an important section of the city wall. They took up their position as morning was breaking and the battle commencing.

Gwinevere and Melleas and Lupus and I were left in the care of a broad-shouldered fellow named Bertilak; Melleas said he was Carmelide's finest swordsman. Safeguarding the prince and princess was an important task, but Bertilak wasn't overjoyed about it; he'd have much preferred to be in the midst of the real action. But if he couldn't be in it, the next best thing was to keep a close eye on it. So it wasn't long before he'd taken the four of us up onto the rooftop of Carmelide Keep, the tallest building in the city. From there we had a splendid view of the whole scary business.

In the early going the action was carried by King Ryence's foot soldiers, who rushed the city walls at about ten

different places at the same time. They threw their long ladders against the walls and swarmed right up them like angry
pismires. Our defenders waited until the attackers were nearly
at the top, and then they shoved against the ladders with poles.
As the ladders teetered backwards, blokes leaped and tumbled
in every direction.

Sometimes the attackers were greeted by rocks the
size of a man's head, sometimes by tubs of boiling water.
Every now and then a few of them actually made it up onto
the walls; then there were sword fights and hand-to-hand combat, little set-tos that usually ended with bodies flying through
the air—some alive and some not.

The whole time the air was thick with arrows. The
city's archers, who were packed into the round guard towers
that stuck out from the city walls, kept up a steady fire on the
attackers. At the same time masses of arrows streamed in
from the Northgalians, who stood in neat rows about a hundred yards from the walls. Some of the city archers shot
through narrow arrow loops or from out on the parapet through
larger openings. That was much riskier, and some of those
fellows paid a heavy price for doing it.

The weakest spot in a city's defenses is its main entrance. That's why there's always a lot of extra stuff protect-
ing the great gateway—portcullises, murder holes,
machiolation—good stuff like that. The main gate of
Carmelide was very well fortified, so it didn't surprise me
that the attackers were steering clear of it. But as it turned
out, that was just a clever ploy. Those wily devils were wait-

ing for our defenders to get all spread out before mounting a massive assault on the city gates.

A couple of hours into the battle a group of Northgalians we hadn't even noticed sprang up out of a ditch and dashed toward the gates. One bunch of them carried a huge battering ram, and another bunch carried a wooden wall that was draped with wet animal skins. The portable wall was supposed to protect the fellows carrying the battering ram, and the wet skins were supposed to keep it from burning. Our men peppered it with flaming arrows, filling the air with a horrible stench.

When the fellows with the battering ram reached the gate, they started bashing away—*bam*! *bam*! *bam*! Even up on top of Carmelide Keep we felt the vibrations, and it wasn't long before the great gates of Carmelide began to buckle. And that's when I noticed that the strong iron grids of the gatehouse were *still up*!

"You flea-brained *idiots*!" I barked, "you gnat-brained *morons*! Lower those *dad-blasted portcullises*!"

Once the massive wooden gates were thoroughly bashed in, the fellows with the battering ram tossed it aside and flattened themselves against the walls, making it harder for our archers to hit them, and out of the ditch poured hundreds of screaming madmen. They made a beeline for the entrance to the city. "Holy Jerusalem!" I thought, "Holy Heavenly Jerusalem!"

When maybe half the attackers had poured through the entranceway and entered the city, that's when I heard the grinding and clanking of chains and saw those great iron grids finally coming down. "Too *late!*" I barked angrily. "Too dad-blasted *late!*"

Then it dawned on me what was really going on. The sly dogs who were guarding the gate weren't as stupid as they looked. Those fellows had pulled the wool over my eyes and over the Northgalians' eyes too, and now the beauty of the defenders' plan became perfectly clear. The attackers had been divided in two, and now the fool-hearty fellows who'd rushed into the city were cut-off from their companions.

In no time at all arrows were whizzing down upon them—from the walls behind them and from the buildings in front of them. The Northgalians didn't stop fighting, but they didn't have the ghost of a chance. In no time at all, those poor blokes bore a distinct resemblance to human pincushions; I even felt a twinge of pity as they struggled on to their inevitable ends.

King Ryence's army was piling up casualties fast, and the Carmelidians were doing a nifty job of saving their own skins. Throughout all of this Arthur's men had stayed put on their own small section of wall, which they'd defended with total success. One time a handful of attackers did make it up to the top, but what bad luck for those poor blighters! By the time our guys got through with them they'd been thoroughly sliced and diced.

While I'd been keeping track of the larger shape of things, my brother's attention had remained fixed on Kei.

Now and then Lupus would let out a yip or a yap to tell me that Kei had just done something wonderful. Lupus *really* got worked up when Kei was hit in the shoulder by an arrow. But after he'd been treated and bandaged up, Kei was back on the wall again, eager as ever to be in on the fight. But the strangest thing was that when Lupus had been all worked up, I'd begun to feel the exact same things *he* was feeling! After the night before, when we'd rescued Lupus from the Northgalians, whenever my brother's feelings were at their strongest, the blasted things were sent right straight into my own little brain. Goodness gracious me, I thought, will wonders ever cease?

Throughout the battle Arthur had done a lot of *watching* but not a single bit of *participating*. Believe me, I was getting a bit irked. It seemed like everybody under the sun was getting in on the glory—so why not Arthur? Besides, all of Lupus' crowing about Kei's heroics was getting on my nerves—*I* needed something to crow about too!

Just as I was thinking that, everything went haywire. Just as I was wishing that Arthur would get more involved, that's when I felt the tremors—a slight trembling to begin with but then a terrible shaking. That was followed by a rumbling noise and an even greater shaking—and then came the horrible *crash*. It seemed as if Carmelide Keep would topple and fall. It didn't, but dust was everywhere—especially in my eyes and nose and throat. And then we heard the cries of men in agony.

It took a minute or two for the dust to start clearing away, and then we could see that a huge section of the city wall was no longer there—it had *crumbled completely.* "Peter, James, and John!" I thought, "can such a thing be possible?" One moment it was there, firm and strong as anything, and the next it was nothing but a gigantic pile of rubble.

"Oh, my Lord!" cried Bertilak. "They've undermined the wall. They'll be in on us like a pack of howling wolves." He was right about that, for Northgalians were already swarming over that great pile of rubble and moving toward the gap in the walls.

IV   *Cleodalis the Magnificent*

Folks in Carmelide seemed stunned. The Northgalians had breached the walls of the city, and no one was doing a blessed thing about it. "Wake up!" I barked. "We're being attacked! They're entering the city! Stinking Northgalians are entering the city!" Where, oh where, were the noble defenders of Carmelide?

Finally someone appeared on the scene, a man who seemed to be Carmelide's only defender. He came charging along the wallwalk to the place where the walls had crumbled. Then he leaped right off the wall and landed on his feet beside that huge pile of rubble. It was a prodigious leap—all the way down from the parapet—but this lone defender of Carmelide had done it. There he stood, all by himself, on his long sturdy legs.

Although he was by himself, perhaps it isn't quite accurate to say he was alone. For cradled in his hands was his precious companion—his long-shafted, double-headed polaxe. He'd no sooner arrived then so did the Northgalians. He stood squarely in their path, this valiant man who was the sole defender of Carmelide.

The Northgalians began swarming around him, but before they could get to him, he was swinging his polaxe in a great swirling circle. Believe me, that stopped his attackers right in their tracks! Then they began spreading out cautiously, staying just out of reach of his whirling weapon. Each time the long-handled axe went past, they made stabbing motions, trying to get at him before his grim weapon came round again. The slower ones, I'm happy to say, soon made the acquaintance of that brave man's companion.

Looking down from Carmelide Keep, we watched in wonder as this magnificent fellow worked his magic. He stood with his legs firmly planted, whirling his wondrous weapon with his muscular arms and shoulders—this one measly man who was holding the entire Northgalian army in check, all by himself.

"It's *Cleodalis!*" cried Melleas, hopping from one foot to the other. "It's *Cleodalis!* And he's whipping the Northgalians all by himself!"

"Yes," came Bertilak's soft reply. "It's Cleodalis— my cousin Cleodalis—my dearest friend in the world."

Unfortunately, this wonder-working fellow couldn't keep this up forever; indeed, he'd already begun to show signs of wearing out. And as he was tiring, his foemen edged in closer, watching for the right moment to deliver a fatal blow.

But before that could happen, this marvelous fellow discovered that he was no longer alone. For just when it was looking grim, a *second* defender came flying down from above—a second defender who possessed a brightly gleaming sword. Quickly he slashed his way through the ring of attackers and took up his position beside the arm-weary Cleodalis. And this second defender was *Arthur*.

Without speaking a word the two men put their backs to each other so they could face their attackers. The man with the polaxe now used it like a spear, jabbing at the chests of the Northgalians with its long sharp point, while Arthur's blade danced in the morning sun. At almost the same time Arthur parried the blows of a pair of Northgalians and then reposted with vicious, effective thrusts of his own.

As we watched the unfolding of this glorious, terrifying event, I was growing more nervous by the second. Arthur, I knew, was in very grave danger. Bertilak was as jittery as I was, for all of a sudden he blurted out, "I'm sorry, but you folks are on your own. Cleodalis is in trouble and I must go to him!"

Bertilak dashed off toward the stairs that led to the lower levels of Carmelide Keep, and without even thinking I dashed right behind him. Running through my little dog brain was a single thought— "My master is in trouble and I must go to him!"

Carmelide Keep was a tall and complicated fortress, and it took us a minute or two to negotiate its staircases and passageways. By the time we charged into the street, things down there had changed. Arthur and Cleodalis weren't blocking the hole in the city walls; they weren't holding the Northgalians in check. Their backs were pressed against a building and ruffians were taunting them and jabbing at them with their swords. Arthur and Cleodalis weren't trying to save the city of Carmelide; they were trying to save their very own *selves*.

Northgalians now poured into the city, streaming down the street in both directions. Bertilak and I couldn't do anything about that, but we could do what we'd come to do—aid the ones we loved most in the world.

Bertilak smashed through that semi-circle of taunting men, his double-edged sword stabbing and slashing. He dispatched one of them with his very first thrust, and with a quick sideways swipe he sent the sword flying from the hand of another.

I hurled myself at the back of the bloke closest to Arthur, sinking my teeth into his partially-exposed neck. The unexpected arrival of a large air-borne canine caused the poor fellow to fall right onto the point of Arthur's blade.

"Enjoy yourself in *Hell*, you stinking swine!" I barked in fury. "Give my regards to Lucifer and his pathetic pals!"

The other Northgalians, seeing that the odds had shifted, decided not to stick around. They scurried off down the street with their flea-bitten tails tucked between their legs.

"*Run*, you cowardly curs!" I barked after them. "If you want to survive, you'd better *run!*"

But surviving wasn't in the cards for them after all. For as they dashed down the street they ran right into a troop of mounted horse-soldiers coming from the opposite direction. No, those poor fellows ended up being skewered by lances or trampled by the hooves of charging warhorses.

Cries and shouts now came from the other direction, where panic-stricken Northgalians were pursued by yet more mounted soldiers. And who should be leading this group of knights but Merlin the Wizard! There he was, loping along on Bryn, his huge black charger, and right beside him was Kei, using Brutus' great bulk to maximum advantage.

The Northgalians began tossing down their weapons and falling on their knees, begging for mercy. It irks me to tell you that they actually got it. Considering all the damage they'd done and the people they'd injured, it didn't seem right that those horrid fellows should get off so easily. Yet there we were—showing them *mercy!* Taking pity on a defeated enemy—that was the *noble* thing to do!

So the Northgalians who were inside the city became our prisoners, and the ones who were outside soon beat a hasty retreat. By evening the entire Northgalian camp, the very same camp we'd come dashing through in the wee hours of the morning, had vanished. The bad news was that they'd left a lot of stinking rubbish behind; the good news was that

King Ryence and the tattered remains of his army were now nowhere to be seen.

Leodegrance's knights pursued them and managed to pick off some of the stragglers. When they got back, they said that King Ryence and the remnants of his army were gone from the land of Carmelide. All I can say is, good riddance to bad rubbish.

As you can imagine, there was a lot of tidying up to do. But I'm happy to say that I slept through most of it. When I went to sleep that night I was tireder than I could remember. I slept all that night and part of the next day. When I finally woke up, there was Melleas, sitting beside me and grinning like anything. Arthur had asked him to keep an eye on me, and that's exactly what he was doing. In fact, he was keeping *two* eyes on me.

After we enjoyed a tasty little snack of cold pasties, Melleas gave me a guided tour of the city. As he showed me all his favorite spots, it was obvious that that little tyke was extremely proud of Carmelide. Why shouldn't he be? It was his *home*. There is nothing wrong with loving your home. For me, home is the Red Castle, where Arthur and I grew up. No matter where we go, the damp and drafty and dear old Red Castle will always be home.

The Northgalian prisoners were soon put to good use, for they were the ones who had to pick up all the stones from the city wall and stack them neatly. They were the ones who had to carry off all the rubble in huge wicker baskets. They were the ones who had to fill in the deep hole they'd made beneath the city wall. They were the ones who had to dig all those graves—graves mostly filled by their own fallen comrades.

There was another thing going on that day that was much, much more to my liking—the preparations for a glorious celebration. Emanating from kitchens all over the city were wonderful smells, the smells of food being prepared for a magnificent banquet. King Leodegrance's great hall was being spruced up for a whale of a party. After my long sleep and my lovely little tour of Carmelide, I was definitely in the mood to be kicking up my heels.

V   A Cup of Kindness

On the wooden gallery of the great hall musicians were making a lovely racket, and in the open area in front of the tables young women in colorful costumes moved back and forth in an intricate dance. At the far end of the hall nimble tumblers flipped and flopped, reminding me of the fish Emrys and Davi used to pull onto the river bank back at the Red Castle; and jugglers in multi-colored outfits tossed red and yellow balls back and forth with astonishing speed. I lay happily beneath the high table gazing at these activities, trying to take them all in.

My brother's attention was fixed on just *one* thing— a juicy bone Kei had nabbed for him from the kitchen. He held it firmly between his paws, and if I inched up too close, he gave me an evil look and a serious growl. I liked the look of that bone, I won't deny it, but when Lupus has a lip-smacking bone in his clutches, it isn't a good time to be messing with the fellow. Besides, I knew it wouldn't be long till I'd have plenty of good stuff to gnaw on myself. I planned to take it slow and savor every little gnaw.

Arthur and Kei stood behind the high table, chatting with King Leodegrance and some of his advisors. One of them, I noticed, had a swollen nose and a lovely black eye. It was the very same fellow Kei had punched in the eye when we'd first arrived at Carmelide—that pompous fool was one of the king's closest advisors! Cleodalis was there too, the man who'd worked wonders with his polaxe. Melleas told me he was the Castellan of Carmelide—whatever *that was!* Next to him was Bertilak, our companion up on Carmelide Keep. But there wasn't a single woman at the high table. That was because Leodegrance was a widower and because his daughter Gwinevere was busy elsewhere overseeing the entire shindig.

There were plenty of women at the side tables, though, and some of them were truly eye-catching. The younger fellows, I noticed, weren't shy about checking them out good, and there was one young woman who was the object of a great deal of attention. She had silver-blond hair and eyes the color of violets. Her neck was as pale as ivory and her cheeks were as pink as a foxglove. Woven through her hair was a delicate chaplet made from purple and white clover, and around her neck hung a silver chain with a large purplish stone. When Melleas saw me gazing at it, he told me it was an amethyst. A lot of eyes were paying tribute to this lovely young woman. But she, I could tell, only had eyes for one fortunate fellow—*Bertilak.* And Bertilak, I could tell, only had eyes for her.

After the priest gave the blessing, King Leodegrance remained on his feet, waiting for folks to shush up. Then he loudly proclaimed, "Let us drink to our glorious king! Let us raise our glasses to Arthur of Britain—our noble, courageous king—who risked life and limb for the safety of Carmelide!" Everyone lifted their goblets and shouted out in unison, "Hail, Arthur, King of the Britons!" Arthur's cheeks turned as pink as those of Bertilak's lady.

As folks were sitting down, it was Arthur's turn to leap to his feet. He raised his goblet and shouted, "Friends, companions, Carmelidians—please join with me in drinking a toast to Cleodalis, the peerless Castellan of Carmelide. When it comes to wielding a polaxe, this noble fellow has no equal in all the land of Logres!" Logres, I didn't need Melleas to tell me, was one of the ancient names for Britain. Merlin always used it, and Arthur had picked up the habit too.

Arthur's toast to Cleodalis brought loud cheers from nearly everyone in the hall. But right at that moment I glanced at Leodegrance, and I couldn't help seeing the sour look that came over his face. Leodegrance exchanged glances with the fellow with the black eye, and *he* had a sour look on his face, too. Now, what in the heck does *that* mean, I wondered? Could it be that the noble King of Carmelide is a wee bit jealous of his very own Castellan?

Just as my patience was wearing thin, we finally got down to the essential business of the evening—*eating*! And whatta ya know, servers were actually bringing stuff straight to Lupus and me. That's what I call running a proper banquet. Gwinevere's doing, no doubt, the kind of thoughtfulness a humble dog like me really appreciates. Arthur was keeping me well supplied with morsels of this and tidbits of that, and one time Melleas came rushing over to say, "Cabal, you really must try these black-currant biscuits!" Yumm. Melleas had a very good point.

Among the entertainers at the banquet was one little fellow I really need to mention; that's because later on he became a very special friend. His name was Dagonet, and he was a lively little minstrel who sang and cavorted and told funny stories. One was about some rude and raucous tools that got into a big squabble with a shiftless carpenter. Dagonet played all the parts in his skit by himself, giving each of the tools its own special voice and personality. Those nasty-tempered tools did a lot of bickering and name-calling, and just as the situation was turning into a drunken brawl, the carpenter's mean tough wife rushed in. She said every one of them was a good-for-nothing loafer; then she chucked the whole lot of them out into the street—including her husband!

As folks were laughing and cheering and Dagonet was making a series of silly bows, I slipped out from beneath the table and took a good look at my master. Arthur, I was relieved to see, had a big silly grin on his face. Lately he'd become a much too serious fellow, but right at that moment he was acting more like his regular old self. Thank goodness for *that*.

And that's when I spotted *another* familiar face—the withered old visage of Merlin the Wizard. Where in blazes had *he* come from? Merlin, being the secretive old bird that he is, usually steers clear of big public gatherings. He's the kind of fellow who prefers the shadows to the bright lights. I knew that something important must've come up to cause him to appear at Leodegrance's banquet.

I slipped over close to him to check him out good. I can learn a lot about what Merlin's been up to by sifting through the smells layered on top of his own peculiar sour-apple smell. First, I got a whiff of Merlin's horse Bryn, which told me he'd been riding. Second, I picked up the smells of gorse and broom, so I knew he'd been riding through rough country. Third, I caught a very faint *person* smell. It was familiar to me, yet I couldn't quite put my paw on it. Hmm. Maybe it would come to me later.

Merlin patted me once or twice and gave me the hint of a smile. A rather lukewarm greeting, but by then I knew the old geezer well enough to know what it meant—something was weighing on his mind. Merlin inched up close behind Arthur and whispered in his ear. Arthur listened closely and nodded his head.

Then Merlin moved wearily toward the end of the high table and plopped himself down beside Bedivere. A serving girl hurried up and filled his goblet, and another one brought him a knife and a plate. But for the rest of the evening Merlin's plate remained empty. He wasn't much interested in eating, but something was sure eating *him*.

It was a little after that that Gwinevere made her only appearance at the banquet. This was during a lull in the fes-

tivities when the entertainers were quiet and most of the servers had left the room. This was the moment Gwinevere had
chosen to enter the hall. And when she did, all the heads in
the room turned in her direction and all the chattering and
clattering came to a halt. Everyone's eyes were on that lovely
young woman. My word, did she ever look grand!

Gwinevere wore a long flowing gown of the palest
shade of yellow. Woven through her dark-brown hair was a
silky ribbon the color of the summer sky. In her hands she
carried a golden cup that shone like the sun; and if that wasn't
enough, it was ringed with gemstones of a deep reddish hue.
"Rubies," Melleas whispered in my ear.

Gwinevere moved slowly down the room, passing
between the side tables. When she reached the high table,
she stopped in front of Arthur and her father. Then she bowed
down before Arthur, her head bent so low that folks could
glimpse the fair white skin on the nape of her neck. When
she lifted her head she gave Arthur a very shy smile.

"My gracious lord," she said, "I would be honored if
you would accept my humble gift." Humble, my eye! There
wasn't anything humble about *that* gift. Arthur looked down
at Gwinevere with a shy little smile of his own, the perfect
match to the one she'd given him.

"My lady," said Arthur, "I am the one who is honored. But I accept your gift with my whole heart. I will
treasure it always."

Gwinevere reached out toward Arthur, holding the
beautiful cup between her hands, and Arthur reached out to

receive it. As he did, he placed his hands on top of Gwinevere's hands. He let them stay there for a few seconds while the two of them looked straight into each other's eyes. Then Arthur slid his hands lower so he was supporting the cup by himself.

Gwinevere's eyes remained on Arthur's a moment longer; then she dropped her gaze and removed her hands from the cup. She gave Arthur a polite little curtsy and then spun around and retreated back down the room the way she'd come. Everyone watched her as she passed through the huge doorway.

"Blimey!" said Leodegrance with a laugh, "my daughter seems determined to give away the family treasures. Well, my lord Arthur, I certainly can't top *that*. But I do have something I think will interest you."

Leodegrance raised his arm and pointed toward the other end of the hall. I had no idea what he was pointing at, and Arthur didn't either.

"It's the *table*," he shouted, "the table hanging on the wall!" Leodegrance was pointing at a large round piece of wood mounted above the doorway through which Gwinevere had come and gone. It was painted in brightly colored bands that radiated out from a golden crown in the center. I'd noticed the thing earlier when I'd given the room the once-over. I'd certainly seen it, but I never suspected for a single moment that the bloomin' thing might be a *table*.

"That's *my* gift to you, my liege," Leodegrance boomed out. "That, and my daughter—if you'll *have* the troublesome girl." Leodegrance was acting very lighthearted about it, but what he'd just done was offer Arthur his daughter's hand in marriage, if Arthur was interested. Knowing Arthur, I didn't doubt that he was. Leodegrance didn't doubt it, either.

"I can't really say the table's a *gift*, Arthur, because you already own it. King Uther left it in my care, and I've always known the time would come when I would need to return it to its proper owner, Uther's successor. But since it's already yours, let me add something else into the bargain— fifty of my finest knights to accompany the Round Table— men I hope will be a credit to your fellowship. And you are free, my liege, to select any man from among all of those in Carmelide."

"Stop!" Arthur said with a laugh, "I need to catch my breath. Gifts are coming at me faster than Northgalian arrows."

Arthur placed the beautiful cup in Sir Lucan's care, and then he and Leodegrance left their seats and walked across the hall to take a closer look at the table. Not wanting to miss out, I tagged along, and so did Merlin. Leodegrance told Arthur how important the table had been to King Uther and how the king, worried about Britain's mounting troubles, had left it with him for safekeeping.

Arthur wanted to know when it was made, who made it, and why it meant so much to King Uther. Leodegrance couldn't answer his questions, but Merlin could. In fact, *Merlin* was the very person who'd designed the table. He'd modeled it after another table that had been used a long time ago at something called The Last Supper. I had no idea what that was, but it certainly sounded grand. *The Last Supper!* What I didn't understand, though, was how any supper could be the *last* supper. Last before *what*, I wondered?

As the three of them were talking, Leodegrance's porter came through the door with two late-arriving guests, a young man and woman. I poked my nose around him to take a look, and then I jumped for joy. Standing there was our old friend Taliesin, along with an attractive young woman I'd never seen before. She was tall and slender and her long flowing locks were as black as a raven's wing. Her large dark eyes sparkled in the torch lights of the great hall.

Taliesin and his companion quickly dropped to one knee before Arthur, but just as quickly Arthur took their elbows and raised them back up again. Then he threw his arms around Taliesin and gave him a big hug; and I stretched out my muzzle and gave Taliesin's long-fingered hands a big lick. My goodness, it was a month of Sundays since we'd last seen Taliesin the Bard.

"My liege," said Taliesin, "allow me to present my cousin Nyneve." The young woman bowed again to Arthur, who once again raised her back up.

"King Leodegrance," Taliesin said, "allow me to introduce my cousin Nyneve. My lord Merlin," Taliesin said turning to Merlin, "I would like you to meet my cousin Nyneve." Nyneve smiled at King Leodegrance and gave him a polite curtsy. Then turning to Merlin she said in a soft gentle voice, "My lord Merlin, I am pleased to make your acquaintance."

For Leodegrance, meeting Taliesin and his cousin wasn't any big deal. To him they were just a pair of unfamiliar guests who'd arrived a bit late for his celebration. But when I glanced over at Merlin, what I saw truly amazed me— for the old geezer's eyes were wide and he was staring at Nyneve. It seemed to me that he was *terrified*! Merlin the Wizard looked truly *terrified*! Now, what in the world was I supposed to make of *that*?

VI Merlin Shows
His Human Side

Taliesin and Nyneve were given seats at one of the side tables, and the rest of us started back towards the high table. My thoughts, though, were entirely on Merlin, for the poor old fellow seemed terribly shaken—something I'd never seen before.

"Merlin," Arthur said under his breath, "I don't understand. What's happened? What's going on?"

Merlin looked terribly forlorn. Beneath his shaggy beard his face looked ashen. He sucked in a big breath and then let it out in the form of a huge sigh.

"Arthur," he said softly, "it seems that my fate just walked through the door."

"What on earth do you mean? Taliesin and his cousin? I don't understand."

"Arthur, *please*," Merlin moaned. "I'll try to explain later when we're by ourselves."

As this exchange was taking place, the two of them had stopped in the middle of the great hall. They stood there face to face. Arthur stared into the eyes of his old teacher. Then he threw his arms around Merlin's shoulders and embraced him. When they finally moved on again, one of Arthur's arms remained around his old friend's shoulders.

Now the servers were circulating through the hall with baskets brimming with fruit and cheese, which meant the eating part of the banquet was nearing its end. But I knew that for a lot of these folks the serious celebrating would be going on for quite a bit longer.

As the folks in the hall were nibbling, munching, or just plain wolfing down their desserts, Leodegrance asked Taliesin if he would be willing to play. "I would be honored," Taliesin replied. Yes, and so would *we*—for when it comes to plinking and plonking on a harp, there's no one better than Taliesin the Bard.

As Taliesin was tuning up, Merlin got up from his seat at the high table and went over to the side table and sat in Taliesin's empty one—*right beside* the young woman named Nyneve. What in the world was *this* all about, I wondered? What in the world was the old geezer up to *now*? Wanting to know, I strolled over and nabbed myself a comfortable spot beneath their feet.

Now Merlin was acting like a completely different fellow from the sad-eyed old coot he'd been just a few minutes earlier. He was chatting with Nyneve as if she were some long-lost friend. He was being cheerful and funny, and he seemed very eager to find out all about her.

Nyneve didn't seem to mind Merlin's personal questions. She was enjoying herself as much as he was, and she was tossing in quite a few questions of her own. In no time at all they were chirping away like a pair of birds on a leafy bough.

From her answers to Merlin's questions, one thing was clear—this young woman had a very smart head on her very shapely shoulders. She told Merlin she'd been raised in a nunnery where she'd been instructed in a great many subjects. She could read Latin and French, and she seemed to know quite a bit about a lot of things that were dear to Merlin's moldy old heart.

As I listened and watched, something began to dawn on me. The look I was seeing in their eyes was a look I'd already seen that evening. It was the very same look I'd seen in the eyes of Bertilak and the lady with the silver-blond hair; it was the very same look I'd seen in the eyes of Arthur and Gwinevere. Holy cats, I thought, will wonders never cease!

And I wasn't the only one who was noticing the sparks flying between Merlin and Nyneve. Arthur kept glancing over at them with a very puzzled look on his face. He could see what was happening and he was just as perplexed as I was.

Then I noticed a fellow seated nearby nudge his neighbor and say with a wink, "Watch out there, old Merlin. You know what they say— 'Late love's worse than lad love'!" The folks around him began to laugh. I guess they thought it was amusing. As for me, I didn't know *what* to think.

The only other thing I want to tell you about the banquet concerns Taliesin's performance. I've heard Taliesin sing on many occasions, and I've never once been disappointed. Sometimes the words to his songs are a little puzzling, but his melodies are always heavenly. But this time he sang something that wasn't like anything we'd ever heard from him. It was a lot more like what you'd expect from a silly minstrel like Dagonet than from a true bard like Taliesin. Anyway, here's what he sang.

> In the City of Carmelide,
>> Not far from the sea,
> There dwelt a bold warrior,
>> A man with *esprit*.
> He could wield a mean polaxe,
> He could hack with the best;
> And though quite short on brains,
>> He was huge in the chest.
> He was known far and wide and known more or less, as—
>> Cleodalis! Cleodalis! Cleodalis the Clueless!
>
> Now high-walled Carmelide
>> Was under fierce attack,
> And King Ryence's swarming minions
>> The city meant to sack.
> The denizens of Carmelide town
>> Were in a hell of a mess;
> Their only chance of survival

With one measly man did rest;
That man, that man, that glorious cuss,
      Was none other than—
Cleodalis! Cleodalis! Cleodalis the Clueless!

Then the walls tumbled down
      And the Smelly Ones came;
But a bold man they found there
      Who was right on his game.
It was Cleodalis the Clueless—
      That mellow, magnificent chap!—
Who hopped down off the walls
      And staunchly filled the gap.
And the first of the Smelly Ones,
      The first of those who came,
Were soon armless or legless—
      No, never quite the same!—
      Thanks to mighty Cleodalis,
      That glorious, brainless cuss—
Cleodalis! Cleodalis! Cleodalis the Clueless!

Taliesin kept right on going like that, dishing out his silly rendition of Cleodalis' heroic deeds. And it wasn't long before everybody in the great hall had gotten into the spirit of the thing. When Taliesin reached the end of each verse, they all raised their mugs and shouted out in unison, "Cleodalis! Cleodalis! Cleodalis the Clueless!"

Cleodalis stood at the high table with his hands on his hips and his head thrown back in laughter. He wasn't offended by Taliesin's song; he knew it was all in fun. King Leodegrance, I noticed, was laughing and smiling along with the rest. I guess it was hard for him to be jealous of someone that everyone seemed to be laughing at.

As I thought about what Taliesin was doing, I realized he was being quite clever. If he'd sung a song that praised Cleodalis, Leodegrance and his supporters might've been miffed. This way he offered a nice little tribute that wouldn't upset anyone. Taliesin, I said to myself, I never imagined that you were such a sly dog.

VII   The Agonies of a Wizard

Melleas was struggling against his need to yawn, but he was losing. And I didn't feel fresh as a daisy myself. It was time for the two of us to be hitting the hay. A lot of the folks had begun to leave the banquet, heading off for their beds, and pretty soon only the hard-core celebrators would be left.

Arthur would be leaving soon too, but I knew he'd be up most of the night having a serious talk with Merlin. I wanted to be in on that conversation, but right now it was more important to accompany Melleas back to his chamber, which was across the street in the great gatetower in the city walls.

King Leodegrance's chambers were in the upper levels of Carmelide Keep, but Melleas and Gwinevere no longer stayed there. Their rooms were in the great double-sided gatetower that surrounded the main entrance to the city. That's also where the choicest guestrooms in Carmelide were and where Arthur and some of his knights were staying. Gwinevere's chambers were on one side of the gatetower, and Melleas' room and the guestrooms were on the other.

Melleas, the lucky little devil, had a spacious chamber all to himself. It was on the floor just below the top floor, and although it had only one small window, it had a large wall painting of knights engaged in a ferocious melee. Arthur's chamber was right below Melleas', and a short flight of steps connected the rooms of my two dear friends, making it was easy for me to dash back and forth.

After Melleas said goodnight to his father and Arthur, we set off for his chamber. When we got there, the tired little guy kicked his boots into the corner and crawled sleepily into bed. I hopped in and snuggled up close. I'd grown very fond of Melleas in the few days that Arthur and I had been at Carmelide. I was almost as fond of the little tyke as he was of me.

Lying there all cosy and snug with Melleas made me think of the times when Arthur and I used to snuggle up together at the Red Castle. Of course, Arthur's little room in the Red Castle wasn't nearly so nice as this one, and Arthur and I usually slept on the floor in a heap of blankets, not in a huge and comfortable bed. But it gave me a good feeling remembering those carefree days of yore—before Arthur and I had the cares of the world dumped on our sturdy young shoulders.

Melleas was soon fast asleep. I shut my eyes for a moment, and the next thing I knew I was waking up from what must've been a solid little dognap. I didn't know how long I'd slept, but I knew it was high time to get myself downstairs and find out what was going on with Arthur and Merlin.

I slithered from beneath the covers and padded softly out of the room. I dashed down the staircase and nosed my way through Arthur's partially-open door. There were my two best friends in the world, deep in conversation.

My word, was Merlin ever agitated! The old duffer was pacing back and forth, waving his arms this way and that. "*Women*," he kept shouting, "why is it always *women* that lead us to our downfalls, Arthur? Over and over it's been women! Why, oh why, did He who made this glorious world of ours ever put *women* in it? Tell me *that*, Arthur, tell me *that*!"

Gracious sakes alive, the old duffer had worked himself into quite a lather. His eyes looked wild and his hair and beard stuck out this way and that. The way he looked right now, no wonder some folks thought he was nothing but a raving lunatic.

"*Come on*, Merlin," Arthur shot back. "How could Nyneve ever harm you? She's a completely innocent young woman. She's kind and gentle and intelligent. She's attractive, too, though I dare say you've noticed *that* on your own."

Merlin seemed caught off guard by Arthur's last remark. "Well, yes," he muttered, "she *is* all those things. But that's the problem, isn't it. Nyneve *is* kind and gentle, intelligent and attractive—a fatal combination, Arthur, a *fatal* combination. That's why I find her so irresistible. Oh Arthur," Merlin implored, "that's why I find her so *irresistible*."

"Why resist, Merlin? Where's the harm in *not* resisting? Surely there isn't anything wicked about her."

"No, of course there isn't anything wicked about her. And I know that in times to come she will do your kingdom much good. But I also know that if I get involved with her it will lead to my destruction. I don't know how or why. There's a fog swirling about that part of my future. But one thing is certain—if I don't stay away from her, it will lead to my undoing."

Merlin looked so forlorn that I just couldn't stand it. I went over and licked his hand, whining softly and looking up at his sad, sad eyes. "Merlin," I said inside my head, "maybe you're wrong. I once heard old King Uther say that sometimes you're wrong. Maybe this is one of those times." Merlin looked down at me and shook his head sadly. "I don't think so, Cabal, I really don't think so. Not this time."

Arthur gave Merlin and me a puzzled look, and then he stepped over to Merlin and put his arms around his shoulders, just as he'd done at the banquet. We both wanted to comfort our dear old friend; neither of us quite knew how to do that.

"Arthur," Merlin said softly, "I'm drawn to her—like the moth to the flame—and there's nothing I can do about it." Arthur held on to Merlin and patted him softly, like a mother pats a wee small babe.

"Merlin," Arthur said after a bit, "a very wise man once told me that where a man's heart is, there shall it be. Gwinevere has *my* heart, and that's where it's going to be. If Nyneve has yours, that's where it's going to be also."

Merlin sighed. "You're right, Arthur, you're right." After a little pause Merlin whispered, "Heaven help us both, my son, heaven help us both."

Fortunately, all this moaning and groaning couldn't go on forever, and eventually the conversation moved on to why Merlin had turned up unexpectedly at the banquet. Merlin pulled out a grimy old handkerchief, wiped around his eyes and blew his nose. Having collected himself, he snatched his old cloak from the bench beneath the window and rummaged about in an inside pocket; he fished out a rolled piece of parchment that was tied with ribbon. I stretched out toward it and gave it a good sniff. And that's when I finally recognized the person-smell that had eluded me earlier—it was *Emrys*! My goodness, I thought, how could I have missed so familiar a smell.

Emrys had been one of Tom kennelman's chief assistants back at the Red Castle, but these days he worked for Merlin. When Sir Ector agreed to let Emrys become Merlin's special helper, old Tom was really irked; he'd always assumed that Emrys would become the head dog-trainer at the Red Castle. Now old Tom would have to find someone else, for now that Emrys had hooked up with Merlin, there would be no getting him back.

"It's from Nentres," said Merlin, handing the parchment to Arthur. "He's in a bit of a panic. He thinks Angus is really going to attack this time; he doesn't think he can hold the Scots in check. Nentres plans to concentrate his forces in his two strongest castles. He's urging you to come north and help him. But listen, Arthur, Emrys doesn't trust Nentres. He thinks this is a trick. There's a rumor that Angus and Nentres have made a secret alliance. And I don't have to tell you how much Nentres has always lusted after the throne."

Arthur drank in Merlin's words. He read through the message for himself and when he finished, he rolled up the parchment and handed it back to Merlin. Arthur came over and knelt down beside me; he scratched behind my ears and rubbed my chest. His hands felt good, though I knew I wasn't at the center of his thoughts.

"Well, Cabal," Arthur said, "it looks like we're going north. If it isn't one thing, it's something else, isn't it?" Arthur rose up and started pacing back and forth across the room, his hands behind his back, his chin buried in his chest. He kept this up for several minutes while Merlin and I waited quietly.

"Okay," Arthur said at last, "here's what I think. We'll set out day after tomorrow before dawn. We'll need to get a message to Emrys immediately. I want him to meet us at Castle Pendragon in Cumberland. We can be there by Friday night, if we get moving. We'll also send a message to Nentres, telling him we'll come as soon as we can, but we'll be vague about the details. I don't want him knowing our routes, where we'll be stopping, or when we're likely to reach him.

"I especially don't want him knowing the strength of our forces. I'll ask Leodegrance to lend me one hundred additional knights, on top of the fifty he's already promised. That will make us stronger than Nentres will expect. We'll travel as a single unit until we reach Castle Pendragon, where we'll divide into two units. I'll take my men and fifty of the borrowed knights north to Carlisle. Kei and Hervey will take our new men and the other fifty borrowed knights across to Durham and then north from there. That way, if Nentres is planning any nasty surprises, we won't walk into them at the same time." Merlin added a few suggestions, and then the two of them got down to dotting the i's and crossing the t's.

As they were talking, I'd begun to get nervous. How would Lupus and I fit into this plan? Since Arthur had become king, Lupus and I had been regular members of his troop; we'd traveled with them everywhere they'd gone. But this sounded like a very different kind of undertaking. This time Arthur's forces would be traveling farther and faster than ever before. It was beginning to sound like this time Lupus and I would be *left behind*.

"Arthur," said Merlin, looking at me out of the corner of his eye, "what did you have in mind for Cabal and Lupus? Will you be taking the dogs, then?"

"Goodness, Merlin, I don't see how we could. We'll be traveling so quickly, I don't see how the dogs could keep up. Perhaps Melleas would keep an eye on them. I hate to leave them," he said, looking at me sadly, "but perhaps that would be best."

Oh, Arthur! I barked angrily. You wouldn't do a rotten thing like *that*, would you? That time you and Kei left us behind at the Red Castle was nearly the death of us!

"Might I make a different suggestion?" Merlin said. "If Cabal and Lupus could tag along as far as Castle

Pendragon, Emrys could take them on to Northumberland and leave them with Brother Blaise. They'd be safe and snug at the friary, yet not so far from you and Kei. Then when you've concluded this business with Nentres and Angus, you could come to the friary and collect them. I'm sure Blaise would be delighted to see you again, Arthur."

"That's *perfect*, Merlin," Arthur said, looking relieved. "And there's nothing I'd like more than to see Brother Blaise. It seems like such a long time since Kei and I were there."

"That's *perfect*, Merlin," I barked joyfully. "I owe you one, my dear old friend!"

"You surely do, Cabal," said Merlin with a wink, "you surely do."

VIII   Danger in
Dark Alleyways

My head was aching from all their talk, talk, talk. So when Merlin asked if I'd like to join him for a late-night stroll, he didn't have to twist my paw.

"C'mon!" I barked, "what are we waiting for?"

"Indeed, my dear Cabal, what *are* we waiting for?" So Merlin and I sallied forth, leaving poor old Arthur behind, still mulling over his plans for the expedition to the north.

Merlin and I hurried down the winding staircase, eager for a taste of cool night air. And clearly we weren't the only ones who had that idea, for just as we reached the doorway, a pair of folks went strolling by. My nose identified them as Taliesin and Nyneve, and I was rather surprised when we didn't go after them. Instead, Merlin led us in the opposite direction, and before long we were deep in a tangled maze of dark little lanes and alleyways. I hoped to goodness the old duffer had some idea of where we were—*I* surely didn't!

After a couple of minutes we rounded a corner and then there we were again, right back on Carmelide High Street. And who should be coming towards us but Taliesin and Nyneve. Merlin, I quickly realized, had taken us on a route specially designed to create this little chance encounter. Merlin, I chuckled to myself, sometimes you really take the biscuit.

The three of them exchanged surprised greetings, and then there was an awkward silence. Finally Merlin, groping for words, said, "Umm, uh, old Cabal here was wanting to stretch his legs a bit; and because the night air was so refreshing, we decided we weren't in any hurry to be going back in." Well, I guess Merlin wasn't bending the truth *too* much.

"Cabal," Nyneve said, kneeling beside me, "I've heard a lot about you." Then she took my muzzle in her soft, clean-smelling hands and began stroking me gently. Believe me, I could get in the habit of being petted as gently as that.

"Taliesin says you're quite the fellow, Cabal. I probably shouldn't tell you this, but he's been working on a song that's just about you."

A song about *me*? My word, wouldn't *that* be something? But which of my many glorious exploits would he be concentrating on, I wondered? And then *another* thought popped into my head. What if he was making up something silly that would embarrass the heck out of me? I didn't want anybody going around singing about a dog named Cabal the Clueless!

Since Nyneve had let the cat out of the bag, Taliesin sheepishly admitted that he really was making a song about me—and he quickly assured me it was a song that "would do me proud." Believe me, *that* was a relief.

I guess you might say that Taliesin and I were a little slow on the uptake, but it finally dawned on us that Merlin and Nyneve wanted to be alone. That's when Taliesin proposed that he and I go off for a little late-night stroll up on the city walls. As it turned out, it was fortunate we did.

Just a few moments later we were up on the torch-lit walls of Carmelide looking out across the city. These were the very same walls I'd seen from that far-distant hilltop just a few nights before; the very same walls on which there'd been ferocious fighting during the assault on Carmelide. But tonight they were quiet, and aside from a few sleepy-looking guards, we had them all to ourselves. We moved along slowly, looking down at the dry moat below us on the outside and at the rooftops of the buildings packed closely together on the inside. The city was dark, with only a glimmer of light showing here or there through the odd window.

Suddenly from below we heard the clatter of boots, and from around a corner tramped a group of heavily armed men. There were about a dozen of them, moving with determination. They didn't notice us watching from above, and I was glad for that, because those fellows made me very nervous.

"Cabal," Taliesin whispered, "we'd best keep an eye on that bunch. There may be some trouble brewing."

Taliesin and I trotted along the wallwalk until we reached a stairway and then descended to the street. "Come on, boy," Taliesin said softly, "sniff those fellows out. We need to know where they've gone."

That was a tall order, as a matter of fact, since the street was teeming with people smells. But by using my ears instead of my nose I could just make out the sound of boots on cobblestones somewhere off to our left. I dashed in that direction, with Taliesin chasing along behind, and in a couple of minutes we had them in view. They were moving stealthily through the back streets of Carmelide, not knowing that a pair of silent ghosts was flitting along behind them.

The place they were aiming for was a dark corner where two lanes came together. That's where they stopped and plotted their mischief. After a hasty consultation, one bunch of them positioned themselves in the shadows by the corner while the other bunch moved off into the darkness of an alleyway. Then they settled down to wait. Taliesin and I, hidden in our own shadowy places, did likewise.

It was four or five minutes later that we heard the footsteps. Some folks were coming down one of the lanes toward the corner, heading right for the spot where the armed men were waiting. Good gravy, I thought, what if it's Merlin and Nyneve? What if those guys are planning to attack them? But then I realized that it couldn't be Merlin and Nyneve, for they couldn't be making as much racket as these folks were making.

Around the corner came four great burly fellows, striding right along, laughing and joking as if they didn't have a care in the world, four late-night revelers going home from the king's celebration. And I knew who they were—it was

Cleodalis, Bertilak and two of their friends. And they had no idea that they were about to be *waylaid*.

Not knowing what else to do, I barked out at the top of my voice, "Watch out! Some no-good filthy swine are waiting for you!"

The sudden barking of a frantic dog put Cleodalis and his friends on the alert. It was a good thing, too, for right at that moment both groups of armed men came bursting from their hiding places. The odds were heavily against our friends, for it was twelve against four—and the twelve were fully armed and wearing mail shirts. I noticed that their leader had a swollen nose and a black eye. It was the very same fellow Kei had punched in the face, the very same fellow who'd sat next to King Leodegrance at the banquet!

Cleodalis and his companions only carried short swords, but thank goodness they had quick wits, quick reflexes, and very stout hearts. I only wished that Cleodalis would've had his polaxe with him—*then* we would've seen some heads fly! Fortunately, he was standing shoulder to shoulder with Bertilak, the finest swordsman in Carmelide.

It was a terribly unfair fight, and as brave and as skilled as our friends were, they were soon in deep trouble. Blood gushed from one fellow's thigh, and another fellow had a badly sliced-up shoulder. Still, Bertilak and Cleodalis gave their foes as good as they got, and before long everyone there had been bloodied in one fashion or another. Suddenly the fellow beside Cleodalis clutched his belly and crumpled to the ground. He was out of the action for good, making the odds even worse for our friends.

Sensing that victory was at hand, the attackers pressed forward. And just as I was fearing the worst, that's when we heard footsteps behind us—and this time it really was Merlin and Nyneve.

"Merlin!" I shouted inside my head, "do something quick or our friends will be killed!"

To my amazement it wasn't Merlin who took swift action, it was Nyneve. Before Merlin even knew what she was doing, she'd snatched his staff right out of his hand, and using her knee, she'd snapped it into three separate pieces. "Here," she said, tossing one piece to Taliesin and one piece to Merlin. As soon as they were grasping them, those pieces of wood turned into three brightly gleaming swords! Holy Jerusalem, I thought—*that's* a pretty slick trick!

"Come on!" Nyneve shouted, "let's go to it!"

If Merlin looked a bit speechless, poor old Taliesin looked truly startled. "Uh, I've never been much of a fighter," he stammered.

"Tonight," said Merlin "you're a fighter!" Sure enough, without even knowing what was making him do it, Taliesin went rushing into the fray right alongside Merlin and Nyneve. I haven't got a sword, I said to myself, but tonight I'm a fighter too! Before you could say Joseph of Arimathea, I crashed into the legs of the attacker closest to me, making him tumble backward over the top of me. He swore at me as I nipped him on his sword hand, causing him to drop his weapon. I snatched it up by its hilt and dragged it off into the dark alley, at which point that fellow decided it was time to get the heck out of there.

Now it was the attackers who'd been put on the defensive. Like the cowardly rotters they were, when they realized they no longer held the upper hand, they were eager to be away. One of them barked out an order, and then what was left of that gang went tearing off into the night.

Cleodalis—who was the one the attackers were mainly after—only had a few minor scratches. Bertilak had a torn sleeve, and blood was oozing through the fabric, but it didn't seem to be anything major. Their companions were more seriously injured, though not as seriously as some of the attackers. One of them was lying completely motionless on the cold cobblestones of the street. It was the fellow with the *black eye*.

Merlin examined the wounds of Cleodalis' friends, doing what he could for them on the spot. Nyneve bent down and had a good look at the man who lay still on the street. When she looked up at Merlin, she shook her head. We knew what that meant—there was nothing left to do for that fellow but drag him off to the churchyard.

When Merlin and Nyneve had done all they could, Merlin began looking all about with a very concerned look on his face. "What about my *staff?*" he said to no one in particular. "What's happened to my *staff?* That was a damned fine staff, that was—a remarkable old piece of hazel. I *loved*

that old staff—we'd been together for *years!*" he said, ac-
companied by what sounded a bit like a sniffle.

"All right, then," said Nyneve with a grin. "Here,
give me your swords." Holding the three swords between
her hands, she flung them into the air. They twisted and turned
in a skyward dance; and just as they were falling, they suddenly fused together into a single piece of wood.   Merlin
snatched it out of the air before it could hit the street, and
then he ran his hands all over it, caressing it lovingly. In a
trice that old geezer looked a great deal happier.

"Thank you most kindly," he said to Nyneve, making
a small bow. "Now I feel whole again. Thank you also for
your quick thinking and for that impressive demonstration of
your magical skills."

"Actually," said Nyneve, "I'm just a novice at such
things. But my teachers always said I showed a good bit of
promise and that I'd reached the point where I needed the
instruction of a true master."

"Yes," said Merlin, stroking his beard, "you certainly
show a good bit of promise. You say you're in need of a true
master, umm? I have my hands rather full right now assist-
ing Arthur. Still and all, perhaps Arthur and I could make
good use of your fledgling skills, if you'd be willing to lend
us a hand."

"Merlin," said Nyneve, "I would like that very much
indeed."

Eventually we set off in search of our long-neglected beds. When I got back to the gate tower, I padded softly into Melleas' chamber and nestled into bed; the little tyke didn't even know I'd been gone.

I slept rather fitfully for what remained of the night. At one point, a noise from below had me up and staring through the small window. Out on the plain before Carmelide a solitary horseman was moving off into the dark. It was Merlin, riding on Bryn. He was on his way to find Emrys to inform him of Arthur's plans.

part II

"Dogs are people too.
They just aren't human."
— *variously attributed*

1   Farewell — and Hail

The next morning folks in Carmelide were all a-buzz. They knew that Arthur and his men were about to leave Carmelide and they knew that one hundred and fifty of Leodegrance's knights would be going with him. They also knew that fifty of those knights would become permanent members of Arthur's troop. They were eager to find out which men would receive that honor.

Folks were equally a-buzz with rumors about what had happened last night. A lot of stories were flying around and most of them were nowhere near the truth. People were saying that someone was likely to be arrested, for the man who'd been killed, the fellow with the black eye, was the captain of The King's Guard. Not only that, he was one of King Leodegrance's most trusted advisors and closest friends.

And folks were buzzing most of all about Bertilak and Cleodalis. Those two fellows had disappeared completely. I hoped nothing bad had happened to them after we'd left them last night.

Around mid-morning all of Leodegrance's knights were assembled in the large open square in front of Carmelide Keep. Arthur and Kei and Leodegrance and some others sat on their horses before them. Arthur had come to choose his new men. Once more King Leodegrance repeated what he'd said to Arthur at the feast, that Arthur could select them from among all the knights of Carmelide. Now Arthur, sitting high on Tawnyfoot, looked out over that large gathering.

My master addressed all of those men in a very loud voice. He described the journey they would be taking, a journey that would be filled with many unknown dangers. He told them he would only accept men who understood what they were committing themselves to and who freely chose to involve themselves in some very dangerous undertakings. Anyone who joined his troop, he said, would have to remain with him for several years, and anyone who had even the slightest doubt shouldn't volunteer. Before they decided, he said, they should also consider their responsibilities to others.

When he'd finished, Arthur sat quietly on Tawnyfoot, giving them plenty of time to weigh the things he'd said. For a while nothing happened. Then, from several rows back in that great mass of men, a pair of large fellows began shouldering their way forward. They stepped out in front of the others, and guess who they were? Cleodalis and Bertilak.

"My liege lord," said Cleodalis, as he and Bertilak dropped to one knee before Arthur, "my cousin and I are completely at your disposal. We would be honored if you would allow us to join your knightly fellowship." Peter, James, and John! Here was the Castellan of Carmelide, the second most important person in the city—a fellow who just a few days ago had given his all to save the city he loved—and now here he was, volunteering to leave his beloved city to go adventuring with Arthur.

Arthur glanced out of the corner of his eye in the direction of Leodegrance, whose face was contracted in an angry scowl. Leodegrance was furious, but that vindictive fellow had boxed himself into a corner, for knights can't go back on their word and that goes double for a king. He'd repeatedly told Arthur he could have *any* man he wanted, and yet everyone there knew the last thing he wanted was for *these* two men to elude his grasp—more than anything he wanted them punished for the death of the fellow with the black eye.

But knowing Arthur as I do, I can tell you that he couldn't've cared less. And in the next moment he announced in a very loud voice, "Sir Cleodalis and Sir Bertilak—welcome to my fellowship of knights. I hope you will accept positions of trust and authority."

"Our gracious liege," they replied, "we humbly accept."

Leodegrance was really steamed. He was looking daggers at the two men, and he was even looking daggers at Arthur, but there wasn't a blessed thing he could do. As Arthur's foster-father Sir Ector used to say when Arthur and Kei were still young lads, he'd made his bed and now he'd have to lie in it.

Right away several of Cleodalis' friends stepped forward and offered their services, and Arthur quickly accepted them. The process of volunteering continued until Arthur had selected forty-nine men as permanent members of his troop. Each one seemed an excellent fellow, and Arthur's band would be stronger for having them. Now the troop was just one man shy of fifty. Arthur needed one last man.

That was when a familiar voice piped up from way back in the crowd. "My lord Arthur, I would be honored if you would have me as your knight."

A very small person worked his way toward the front of the crowd, and as he did, folks nudged each other and smiled. When he emerged from the crowd, he stood proudly before Arthur, his head held high. Arthur, with his chin in his hand, looked down from Tawny and considered the fellow. Grinning cheerfully he shouted out so that everyone could hear, "Sir Dagonet—welcome to our fellowship of knights. You are our fiftieth warrior! And though the last to be chosen, perhaps you will prove first in courage and prowess."

"Perhaps I *shall*, my liege!" shouted Dagonet in bold reply, "perhaps I shall. When push comes to shove, more than likely I *shan't*. But until a man's mettle has been tested, who's to say?"

We were up the next morning before sunrise. All of Arthur's men—old, borrowed, and new—were assembled before the gates of Carmelide, and a lot of folks were there to see us off. Gwinevere's eyes glistened with tears, and Arthur looked sad too. Once Arthur was mounted on Tawnyfoot, Gwinevere reached up and placed her hand upon his. "I will miss you terribly," she said. "I will miss you, too," Arthur replied, smiling sadly. "But you will be with me in my heart."

Right at that moment a sleepy-looking Melleas came rushing up, his uncombed hair sticking out this way and that. "I'm going to *miss* you, you dear old mutt," he said. He threw his arms around my neck and gave me such a gigantic hug I thought my eyes would pop out of my head! "You won't forget me, will you?" he sniffed. Right away I licked his face and neck, letting him know I wouldn't forget him. "Oh, how I wish I had a sweet lovely mutt like you," he whispered in my ear. "I could really love a sweet lovely mutt like you."

"Woof, woof, woof," I barked, letting him know that I understood what he was saying. Melleas gave me a final little pat. Then he spun around and hurried off, rubbing his nose and eyes with his sleeve.

Then we set off—Arthur's Mighty 200—a very impressive company indeed. When we'd first ridden into Carmelide a few days ago there'd only been fifty of us, and I'd been very nervous about what might happen to us. Now I felt almost cocky, for now we were a fighting force to be reckoned with.

That day we traveled farther and faster than ever before. I've been on some long marches in my time, but nothing that came close to that one. When we finally stopped, my poor old paddy paws had taken more painful pounding than they could handle.

In the cool of the evening, as the men in Arthur's troop were getting themselves settled, I sought out the shallows of a small stream that ran beside the meadow where we'd camped. Easing down into the chilly waters, I gave myself a thorough soaking, and soon the aches and pains of my worn and weary body were being gently soothed away. Quite close beside me a neat little clump of fragrant-smelling grass was sticking out over the water; it was *beckoning* to me. By stretching my neck I could just reach it. That's when a gentle, grass-eating dog treated himself to a tasty and restorative snack.

The next day we rushed along at a furious pace, and about mid-afternoon dark clouds began billowing up in front of us. Wet weather was brewing and we were headed straight for it. It didn't concern me much, for a gentle little shower would cool things down quite nicely.

It wasn't long before I had a serious change of heart, for what was pelting down on us was no gentle little shower! To tell you the truth, I wasn't quite sure what *was* pelting down on us. But it wasn't *gentle*.

"Blimey!" someone exclaimed, "it's a blinking hail storm."

"*I'll* say it's a hail storm! Them balls of hail are big as cherrystones! I think they're making dents in my poor old noggin!"

"A few more dents in *your* noggin, old chap, would be an improvement!"

Those hard little balls flying down from the sky were pellets of *ice*—pellets of ice that stung like hornets. Believe me, getting bashed and battered by hailstones wasn't much to my liking. After about thirty seconds, Lupus and I dashed off the road, heading for the shelter of the outstretched branches of a huge chestnut tree, where we hunkered down in safety while those hard little hailstones kept on pattering and splattering around us.

As the hail collected on the ground, it looked a bit like snow. But we weren't fooled by how it *looked*. That stuff wasn't any soft gentle snow—it was cruel, nasty pellets of *ice*.

Hailstorm or no hailstorm, Arthur and his men kept right on slogging along, a sight which was pretty unnerving for Lupus and me. Fortunately, we weren't entirely deserted, for one of the fellows in the troop had spotted us taking cover. Tugging on his reins, he loped over to join us.

"I'll be staying with the dogs!" he shouted. "We'll catch up later!" The dog-loving knight, we soon discovered, was little Dagonet, the very last fellow to join Arthur's troop.

"Well, lads," he said as he dismounted, "I trust you won't be mindin' a bit of company. To be honest, hailstorms ain't exactly *my* cup of tea, neither."

Dagonet looped his horse's reins around a branch and settled in between Lupus and me, who were sitting upright on our haunches, nervously eyeing all that rapidly accumulating hail. Dagonet draped his arms over our backs and tickled our sides, and Lupus and I gave him a good face-licking on both sides of his face—it was synchronized licking, if you know what I mean—our way of letting him know we appreciated his being there. To tell you the truth, watching Arthur and his men disappear down the road was not a happy sight.

Dagonet assured us that hailstorms never last very long, and while we waited for it to blow over, we huddled together beneath the widespread branches of the chestnut tree. That's when our companion began humming a tune. He hummed for a bit and then he began to sing, fitting words to the tune as he went along:

Hail,

    Hail,

        Hail, hail, hail!

Put it in a bucket

Or put it in a pail;

Put it in a tub

Or weigh it on a scale;

Anyway you slice it, it's

        Hail, hail, hail!

Tink,

    Tink,

        Tink, tink, tink!

Plink,

    Plink,

        Plink, plink, plink!

Tink, tink, tink!

        Plink, plink, plink!

Anyway you slice it, it's

    Hail, hail, hail!

We thought it might rain,

We thought it might snow,

We thought it might freeze,
We thought it might blow,
We thought it might thaw,
We thought it might gale,
And what did we get but
                    Hail, hail, hail!
Hail,
        Hail,
                Hail, hail, hail!
Put it in a bucket
Or put it in a pail;
Put it in a tub
Or weigh it on a scale;
Anyway you slice it, it's
                    Hail, hail, hail!

About ten minutes later, when the hail-spewing clouds had moved off to torment some other folks and *their* unsuspecting dogs, the three of us got back on the road. We got our furry little backsides moving as fast as we could make them move, for if we were going to catch up to our mates before dark, we had to make tracks like we'd never made them before.

Catching up to Arthur's troop wasn't easy, for while we'd been waiting out the storm, they'd kept right on chugging along. It wasn't until the last remnants of daylight were fading from the western sky that we finally glimpsed the troop of riders.

My goodness, if I'd been worn and weary the night before, it was nothing compared to what I felt *that* night. *That* night I was weary from the tip of my wet little nose right down to my well-worn toes.

Fortunately, the next day turned out to be a lot easier for Lupus and me. We'd covered such a great distance the first two days that by mid-afternoon of the third day we'd come within sight of Castle Pendragon. And what a welcome sight it was. I'd had visions of having to push on into the gloom of evening with my body growing ever more weary and my tummy growling ever more hungrily. Thank goodness that wasn't how it turned out.

Our bodies were still plenty weary, but it could've been worse. As for our tummies, the folks at Castle Pendragon had anticipated our needs. They'd even guessed what a couple of foot-sore mutts like Lupus and I might want to gnaw on. In no time at all we plopped ourselves down before platters of juicy venison bones, bones that someone had set aside just for us.

That someone, I soon discovered, was Emrys. For just as Lupus and I were licking the last bits of juice and gravy from the fur around our mouths, there was Emrys, come to greet us. And would you look at the fellow! Why, Emrys had begun to look like *Merlin*—like a youthful version of *Merlin*! He was sporting a full beard now, the first he'd ever had. His hair was shaggy and wild looking—just like

Merlin's. He even had a rather strange look in his eyes, along the lines of Merlin. All he needed now were hands that smelled like sour-apples, and he'd be all set.

Emrys made sure Lupus and I had everything we needed, and then he disappeared again, off to talk with Arthur. I was ready to disappear myself, off to some cosy corner where I could hit the hay. Those three hard days on the road had been no picnic for Lupus and me. We'd made it. We were here. But man, were we *bushed*.

II   Who are *those Guys?*

Arthur and his men didn't stay long at Castle Pendragon, but they did remain there for one full day, catching their breaths, finalizing their plans, and preparing for another long ride. Lupus and I, though, got to laze about. Still, always in the back of my mind was the terrible thought that after tomorrow Arthur would be gone.

Our farewells the next morning were even harder for us than the ones we'd said back at Carmelide, because this time Lupus and I were saying farewell to our masters. The pain of saying goodbye to Arthur is something I've never gotten used to. I knew he had to be off about his business; I knew it was important business; I knew I'd be a hindrance if he took me along. Yet deep in my heart I didn't want him to go. I didn't ever want Arthur to go.

But Arthur went. And so did Kei. So did Sir Bedivere, Sir Lucan, and Sir Griflet. So did Hervey and Sagramore, Cleodalis and Bertilak and Dagonet. Only Emrys remained behind. Good old Emrys. Good old Merlin-looking Emrys.

The plan for Emrys and Lupus and me was to rest up another day and then start off on a northeastward trek across the middle of Britain. We'd be heading toward Durham, just as Kei's troop was doing now, but since we'd be starting a day later and would be moving at a snail's pace compared to them, there wasn't much chance we'd run into them. Still, Lupus could always hope. I took comfort in just knowing that some of our companions would be close by—even if Arthur wasn't one of them.

So on the morning after Arthur and the others had set out, it was our turn. Emrys put his saddlebags onto the back of Pwyll, his steady, uncomplaining horse, and then we were off. Our hearts were still heavy from the farewells of the day before, but soon the journey began to occupy our thoughts. The good news was that now we didn't need to be rushing along. Arthur's men had good reason to be moving quickly, since they hoped to catch King Nentres off guard. But we had no particular schedule to keep and thus no reason to strain ourselves. Our destination was the little friary on the Northumbrian coast where Brother Blaise lived. That's where we were headed, and we would get there when we got there.

It was hard being without Arthur, *terribly* hard. But seeing Emrys again helped make me feel a little better, for Emrys has always been one of my favorites. I'd liked him from the very beginning, back at the Red Castle when he was one of Tom kennelman's helpers. He'd had a knack for training dogs, and Tom had given him the task of shaping up frisky young wise guys like Lupus and me. One time he went with us on an excursion into the Forest of Dean. That was the time Arthur was attacked by a wild boar. Another time he traveled with us to London. That was the time he wolfed down some poisoned chowder that was meant for Arthur. Merlin

saved Emrys' life—with a bit of help from you know who—
and since then Emrys has really been devoted to Merlin. I
guess that's what happens when someone saves your life.

After our adventures in London, Merlin latched on to
Emrys and whisked him away somewhere. When Emrys
didn't come back to the Red Castle, old Tom kennelman was
fit to be tied. He called Merlin every nasty name in the book.
But Merlin claimed he had to have a younger fellow to help
him out. "I'm getting too old, Arthur. I can't do what I need
to without a good bit of help." As far as I could tell, Merlin
hadn't aged a day. He was still the toughest old bird I'd ever
met. No, Merlin had reasons of his own for wanting to latch
on to Emrys—reasons I didn't *yet* fully understand.

Our first two days after leaving Castle Pendragon were
much the same. We'd get off to an early start, move along at
a steady clip till we'd gone six or eight miles, and then we'd
have a nice little rest break. We kept that up throughout the
day—travel, rest, travel, rest—and then in the evening we'd
find a good spot to stop for the night. It was a fairly demand-
ing regimen, but a far cry from what we'd had to do during
the journey from Carmelide to Castle Pendragon.

On the third day things changed. Until then we'd been
on a main road angling northeast toward Durham. But that
morning Emrys turned Pwyll's head off to the left and led us
onto a small track that pointed straight north. Emrys said it
was a shortcut.

"It's one of the ancient trackways," he told us. "Folks
don't use 'em much anymore. Long ago they were Britain's

main roads. The Old Ones used them, the folks who lived here before our ancestors came. They're mostly gone now, except for a few. Actually, you dogs are well acquainted with one of them," he said with a grin. "If you think about it, you'll know who I mean."

I *did* think about it, and I *didn't* know who he meant. Who did I know who could be one of the Old Ones? About the only old geezer *I* knew was Merlin. Was *that* who Emrys was talking about? Was Merlin one of the *Old Ones?*

We went quite a distance that day on the ancient trackway, which wound along on top of a chain of connected hills. Most of the time we were above the tree line, and sometimes we could see far into the distance. At one point I looked off and saw a large cloud of dust rising skyward. Emrys had seen it too.

"Riders moving quickly," he said. "Quite a large group—possibly Kei and his men." Lupus' ears pricked up at hearing his master's name, and he looked at Emrys eagerly. "No way to tell from here, but we'd best be minding our own business. I'm guessing there are *some* riders out there we wouldn't want to be running into."

Before long we'd lost sight of the dust cloud, and along with it went our hopes of seeing some familiar faces. Those hopes were soon replaced by a very keen desire for food and rest. The day was wearing on and our feet were wearing out. Emrys seemed as eager to find a place to stop as we were.

As we were coming down a gently sloping stretch of the track, off to our right we saw wisps of smoke rising above the trees. Probably a small village was tucked away over there. If so, we might find food for our bellies and shelter for our heads.

We turned onto a small path that branched off from the ancient trackway, and in a few minutes the delicious aroma of roasting meat came wafting through the pines. For a pair of hungry, foot-sore dogs, there aren't many things more inviting than that particular smell.

There wasn't a whole lot to the place. A handful of thatched cottages clustered around a square, with a small stone chapel on one side and a bustling little inn on the other. It was the inn that drew us, for that's where the delicious smells of dinner were coming from. Emrys tied Pwyll to a handrail beside a great many other horses; then we went inside to try our luck.

It seemed kind of strange that this small little inn in this out-of-the-way village would be such a lively place, but it certainly was. The room was jam-packed with more plank tables than it could comfortably hold, and every table was occupied by a group of raucous men. Emrys, clutching a mug of ale he'd been handed, found a spot for himself on the floor where he could lean back against the wall. Lupus and I flopped down on each side of him, sniffing the air eagerly and waiting with as much patience as we could muster. This must've been our lucky day, because the hard-working innkeeper, who was scurrying around like a madman attending to everyone's needs, didn't ignore our needs, either. Lupus and I only had a few moments to wait before each of us was in possession of a well-cooked mutton bone.

It didn't take a genius to figure out that the men crowded into this little inn were the very same riders whose dust we'd seen from up on the trackway, for it was clear these fellows had been riding long and hard. That put an end to our hopes that we might run into Kei and his men. But it also left us wondering who in the world these fellows were.

While I gnawed away at my mutton bone, I kept an ear cocked for anything I might pick up from what was being said around us. Emrys sat there quietly, his back against the wall, his eyes closed, his hands cradling the mug of ale from which he sometimes sipped. But Emrys had *his* ears cocked too, just the same as me.

"Where's Rackley, then?" a man said grumpily. "He was s'pposed to meet us here."

"I've never trusted that little weasel," said another. "What's he playing at, anyway? Is he Lot's man or Nentres'? Or is he playing some game of his own?"

"Lot's man or Nentres'!" scoffed the first speaker. "Rackley's nobody's man but Mammon's. He'd cheerfully stick a knife in your back or mine, if there was a profit in it. That's our friend Rackley!"

"No, he's not the fellow to turn your back on," replied the second man, "or to travel alone with on a dark night." Goodness, I thought, whoever this Rackley is, he certainly sounds like a nasty piece of work—if that's how his *friends* talk about him!

It wasn't long before there was a little commotion outside and then a stomping of feet as more men began forcing their way into the overcrowded room. Loud greetings made it clear these newcomers were the ones the others had been waiting for—including the fellow they called Rackley.

I wasn't able to get a very clear view of them at first, because the men on the benches had risen to their feet to greet the new arrivals. But I was anxious to get a good look at them, especially this Rackley fellow, a bloke who was capable of stabbing a friend in the back. As people made room for the newcomers, I finally got a good look at the face of that horrid fellow. And what I saw was a pair of beady eyes, a long pointy nose, and a little rat chin. It was the sharp pointy face of a stinking piece of vermin—for this fellow Rackley was a man with whom I'd had dealings before. This fellow Rackley was none other than my most hated enemy—the rat-faced man!

III   A Spite-Filled Night

What was he *doing* here? How did he *get* here? He was supposed to be locked up tight in the Tower of London. Did he *escape*? Considering how slippery the little turd was, that seemed the likely explanation. The rat-faced man must've escaped from the Tower of London!

A space was cleared at one of the tables for Rackley and the leaders of the men who'd been waiting for him. That was when Rackley glanced over in our direction and spotted Emrys and Lupus and me. Intense hatred poured into his face. His eyes filled with malice, his lips curled in a snarl, his hands became white-knuckled fists. Emrys, knowing that my gorge was rising, laid one arm over my back and gripped my collar. "Easy, Cabal," he whispered, "easy."

"Get those filthy beasts *out* o' here!" Rackley shouted, pulling a knife from beneath his cloak. "Get 'em *out* o' here— unless you want to see 'em dead!" Emrys, with a firm grip on my collar, jumped to his feet, and so did Lupus and I, preparing ourselves for any eventuality.

"Calm yourself down there, Master Rackley," another man said. "Them dogs be well-mannered enough. Them've caused na problems here. Them's mickle good dogs, them two is."

"Get them *out* of here!" Rackley shouted again. "Get them *out*! Or I'll be stickin' 'em with me sticker—startin' with that ugly reddish-brown one!" And he pointed the tip of his blade right at me. Ugly? The man was calling *me* ugly? The man with the face of a *rat* was calling *me* ugly?

"We'll be takin' ourselves off, then," said Emrys. "We're after causin' no problems here." Gripping our collars, he dragged Lupus and me toward the door.

As Emrys was pulling us through the crowd, I heard one fellow whisper to the man beside him, "Rackley's terrible a-feared of dogs, he is; ever since one bit him real good down in London town. They say the teeth marks're still there on his leg, plain as your face." Hearing those words brought a big smile to my heart. I'd have given anything to get a glimpse of those teeth marks. After all, they were the record of one of my proudest achievements.

The good-hearted innkeeper met us at the door with words of apology. He held out a large joint of meat and a loaf of freshly baked bread.

"Make yourselves comfortable out in the stable, if you've a mind to," he said, putting a hand gently on Emrys' shoulder. "The night will na be so chill, and the straw in the loft is fresh and ample." Emrys thanked him and handed him some coins. Then we turned our backs on the inn and our greatly beloved friend the rat-faced man.

Behind the inn was a large outbuilding that served as stables, blacksmith shop, and tool shed. Emrys put Pwyll in a stall, and then he sat down on a stump outside the open door of the blacksmith shop. That's when the three of us lit into the food the innkeeper had given us. Emrys sliced strips of meat off the joint, and the three of us wasted no time in wolfing them down. When the meat was gone, Lupus and I crunched on the bones while Emrys ate thick slices of bread. (I was happy to see he'd put half the loaf away for tomorrow's breakfast.) We washed down our fine repast with cold water from the stream that burbled along behind the stables.

An ancient blacksmith was toiling away inside the little shop. Now, blacksmith shops are among my least-favorite places—ever since I got scalded in one back at the Red Castle. I was just a young pup then, but it made a lasting impression on me. Since then I give places like that a very wide berth. Let's face it, bad things can happen in a blacksmith shop.

Anyway, this blacksmith was a kindly old fellow, and Emrys was soon chatting away with him. Emrys, I'm pretty sure, was trying to pick up bits of useful information, but the old duffer didn't seem to know about anything beyond horseshoes, buckles, and iron spikes—but he sure could prattle on about horseshoes, buckles, and iron spikes.

The innkeeper was right in thinking that the loft in the outbuilding might suit our needs. After the blacksmith finished his chores and trundled off home, the three of us climbed some rickety stairs up to the loft. Lupus and I sniffed and pawed around a bit, and then, being very tired, we burrowed down deep in the straw. Before long, Lupus and I were off in slumberland.

Emrys, however, didn't follow our example. Maybe he suspected the events of the evening weren't quite over. If he did he was right, for sometime later in the night I was awakened by voices coming from beneath us. Torchlights flickered, casting shadows up along the walls and rafters. Several men had gathered there, I guess to hold a private conversation.

Emrys, I noticed, was staying well back in the shadows of the loft, but he was listening carefully to what the men were saying. Unfortunately, my curiosity was getting the better of me. And dumb bunny that I sometimes am, I just had to stick my big nose out from the edge of the loft to get a better look at what was going on. In doing that, I knocked a few pieces of straw over the edge—and they tumbled down onto a man's head. And that man was *Rackley*!

The rat-faced man looked up, and our eyes met. We glared at each other with mutual loathing. At last Rackley managed to wrench his little rat-eyes away from mine. Then he darted them about the blacksmith shop until he found what he was looking for.

Rackley stepped over to the fire and placed his gloved-hand on the cool end of a burning-hot poker. He pulled the poker out of the fire and held it high in the air. It glowed with a reddish-gold glow. A horrible grin spread across his hideous mug. All eyes were on him as he walked over to the stair steps that led to the loft. One thing was very clear to me—the man called Rackley, my most hated enemy, was coming for me.

94

Emotions boiled up inside me like a heavy-lidded caul-
dron getting ready to explode. This was the rotter who'd
crept into Arthur's chamber in the middle of the night and
tried to kill my master. This was the vicious swine who'd
attacked Arthur and Gwinevere beside the River Thames. This
was the stinking piece of slime who'd tried to kill Arthur
with a crossbow in St. Paul's Square. This was the fellow
whose leg would bear the marks of my teeth till his dying
day. But this was also a violent and vindictive man, and he
was grasping a weapon that struck fear to my heart. If I stood
my ground and fought him, as I fully intended to do, I would
probably pay a heavy price—perhaps I'd lose an eye, perhaps more than that.

Rackley was nearing the top of the steps. I could see
the torch light reflecting off his sharp little teeth, for his lips
were pulled back in a hideous grin. This stinking piece of
slime, I realized, was enjoying what he was putting me
through.

"Come on, dog," he hissed through his teeth. "You'd
like to get your teeth into my leg, wouldn't you? I know you
would. So why don't you just come on and try?"

The other men in the room stood rooted right where
they were, oddly captivated by this strange confrontation between man and dog. But if their sympathies lay with the dog,
as you'd naturally suppose they would, they did little to show
it.

I pulled back into a half-crouch, getting ready to pro-
pel myself forward. My teeth were bared too—though *not*

for the purpose of grinning. Rackley, with one hand gripping the railing and one hand holding the burning poker, was almost level with me now. The moment of truth was at hand.

Just as I was preparing to hurl myself at my most detested enemy, Emrys began chanting a strange little chant— "*ignus ignus, lignus flagrare; lignus lignus, ignus cremare*"— or some crazy thing like that. Emrys' chant caused me to hesitate. What on earth was he doing? Emrys murmured his odd little "*lignus, ignus*" chant three times. And that's when the rat-faced man let out a squeal of surprise. Rackley wasn't staring at *me* any more—he was staring at the red-hot poker he held in his gloved hand. What he was staring at was the burning red glow on the end of the poker, a burning red glow that was spreading slowly along the shaft of the poker—right toward his hand!

For a moment the rat-faced man seemed stupefied. He stared as if entranced as more and more of the poker turned reddish-gold. Then he screamed out in pain, for the heat had burned through his glove and into the flesh of his hand. Rackley shook his hand desperately, trying to drop the poker, but he couldn't seem to get it loose from his seared flesh. Finally he shook it free. It fell down to the floor of the shop, where a few small flames flared up from bits of straw lying on the dirt floor.

Clutching his injured hand in front of his chest, Rackley stumbled down the steps and tumbled onto the floor. Then he clambered to his feet and rushed frantically toward the blacksmith's huge vat of water. He plunged his arm in up to his shoulder, all the time making high-pitched squeals and squeaks. The other men shot nervous glances at Emrys and me, especially at Emrys. They weren't sure what he'd done, but they knew darn well it was Emrys who'd caused Rackley's grief. I could tell they were itching to get away fast—in case Emrys took a notion to do something bad to them.

They hurried him off to the inn in search of help. When they were out of sight, Emrys said we'd better be taking ourselves off too, before things started heating up for *us*. A few moments later we were slinking away alongside the stream behind the stables. But as a matter of fact, a couple hundred yards was all the farther we went. When we were safely out of sight among the trees, Emrys made us stop.

"This is far enough," he said. "We'd better keep track of those riders Rackley was talking to. There's some nasty business afoot, more than likely involving your masters. Rackley gave those men information. And if I don't miss my guess, they're King Nentres' men. They've been scouring the countryside, looking for Arthur's troops."

I was beginning to realize that this young friend of ours—this Merlin-looking, Merlin-acting young friend of ours—usually knew exactly what he was talking about.

IV   Ambush!

A few hours later the riders set out from the inn. We slipped from our hiding place and followed after them. The riders rode fast, paying scant attention to what was behind them. That gave us a measure of safety, though if they had noticed us, we could've pretended to be innocent folks who just happened to be going in their direction.

They were soon moving at a fierce clip, so we stepped up our pace also. But after an hour of that Lupus and I had had all we could take, so Emrys made us stop and rest. Over the long haul, dogs can't keep up with horses. After our rest break, we traveled at a speed more suited to our capabilities. We'd lost sight of the riders but it wasn't difficult to follow their tracks.

Late in the afternoon we caught up with them. As we crested a high hill, we could look out before us and see an impressive vista of hills and valleys receding into the distance. We didn't spend much time admiring the view, though, for at the bottom of the hill were the riders we'd been trailing.

Also at the bottom of the hill, sparkling in the afternoon sun, was a broad river. On both sides of the river several narrow tracks angled down to a shallow fording place, which was obviously a major crossing point in the river.

We halted near the top of the hill, standing in the shadow of a huge rock that jutted up beside the track. Shielded from the sight of the men below, we watched them. The riders clustered about their leader who sat high on his horse in the shallow waters of the ford. He was giving them instructions. He pointed his arm across the river and then pointed back in our direction. When he gestured towards us, I was afraid he'd seen us peeking out from behind our rock. But that wasn't it at all. He was showing the different groups of men where he wanted them to take up their positions.

About half the riders splashed across the ford and disappeared among the trees. The rest started up one of the tracks on our side of the river—not our track but another one that angled down to the river not far from ours. In a few moments they'd disappeared from sight. It seemed as if those men had vanished. But they *hadn't* vanished. They were there all right, lurking in the bushes. But for anyone approaching the ford, it would be impossible to know that men were lying in wait.

"Just as I feared," Emrys whispered. "They've set a trap. And who do you suppose they're after? I'm afraid the answer to that one is easy. The tougher question is, what are *we* going to do about it?"

Maybe half an hour later a lone rider came hurrying along one of the trails that angled toward the river from the southeast. As he approached the ford, he made hand signals to the men he knew were hiding on our side of the river. He splashed across the ford and disappeared among the trees on the other side. He was a scout for the fellows waiting in ambush.

Only a few minutes later, a pair of riders appeared on the same trail. I recognized them right off—they were two of the fellows Arthur had chosen at Carmelide. One of them stopped at the top of the hill and watched as his companion went down to the river. When he reached the ford he dismounted and studied the ground. I don't think he liked what he saw, because he kept glancing around nervously.

Holding his horse's reins, he began walking back up the trail, his eyes still on the ground. He was about halfway up the hill when he was waylaid.

Kei's two scouts met similar fates at the very same time. While the fellow down on the trail was becoming target practice for the archers hidden among the trees, the fellow at the top of the hill was yanked from his horse and set upon by four or five attackers. It was a terrible thing to watch, but there wasn't much we could do about it.

Maybe fifteen minutes later Kei and his men appeared at the crest of the same hill. They halted high up on the track and looked down toward the ford. Since his scouts hadn't reported back, Kei would surely be taking every precaution, wouldn't he? He surely wouldn't lead his men straight into a trap, would he? Kei can be foolhardy but he wasn't completely stupid, and I don't think he would have led his men into that ambush. But we never got the chance to find out.

While Kei was sizing up the situation, Emrys took the decision out of Kei's hands. Leaping up onto the rock we'd been hiding behind, Emrys sounded his hunting horn. In a split second that lovely river valley echoed with ear-shattering blasts—"Tur-rah, tur-rah, tur-rah! Tur-rah, tur-rah, tur-rah!" Emrys was blowing "Rechase," the call the Master of the Hunt sounds at the end when he's calling all the hunters and dogs back to their starting point.

To the sounds of Emrys' horn were soon added other sounds—the whiz of arrows in flight—for the archers in the bushes were zinging arrows in our direction. I could hear men moving through the trees, coming up the hill towards us. But Emrys' intention of warning Kei's men had been achieved. They were already off their horses and fanning out among the trees. Soon they were moving down the hill toward the river, flushing out their hated foes.

Now it was the ambushers' turn to be in trouble, for they were pursued by a large and experienced troop of warriors. Abandoning their hiding places, they scurried toward the river—*all* of them, even the ones who'd started up the hill towards us. Fearing for their lives, they splashed across the river to join their companions. At the bottom of the hill Kei's troop regrouped, mounted their horses and charged across the ford in pursuit of their would-be ambushers who were heading for the hills.

Lupus and I watched and listened as the two groups of men, one fleeing and one pursuing, receded into the distance. They went over the next hill and dipped into a valley where they were lost to our sight. Then once more the three of us were alone. That's when Lupus and I turned our attention back to Emrys. There he was, sprawled out on top of the rock, lying in an ever-widening pool of blood. One arrow was embedded in his thigh and another had hit him in the shoulder; its point was sticking out of his back.

V   At Death's Dark Door

That night Lupus and I remained on the rock beside Emrys. We licked at his wounds and licked at his face. When the chilly night air settled down upon us, we snuggled up close against Emrys' body, the three of us sharing our warmth as best we could. For once in our lives Lupus and I didn't think about food; neither of us was the least bit hungry. Maybe we weren't hungry, but we were very frightened. Our friend and companion was horribly injured, and I knew there was a good chance he would die. I wished I could help, but I didn't know how.

The night dragged past and the morning came. But the dawn brought little hope. Emrys was still unconscious, though from time to time he moaned. The bleeding from the arrow wounds had stopped and the blood had dried in ugly-looking clots. Lupus and I no longer licked at them. Emrys needed serious attention, and he needed it soon. Now adding to our despair were our pangs of hunger.

We were in a remote area of northern Britain, but surely there were people around who would turn up pretty soon. Yet all that day not a single person came along our trail. Maybe those folks had been frightened by the clash between the two troops of men. Maybe they preferred to steer clear of trouble. The one thing that did happen was that birds began to gather. Rooks and crows, in particular.

The keen interest of those birds meant that the bodies of Kei's two scouts still lay in the bushes where they'd fallen. Those crows were interested in a meal that was theirs for the taking—and I suspected they were interested in Emrys, too. But the presence of two rough-looking dogs was enough to ward them off, at least for the time being. When the other bodies had been picked clean, no doubt those birds would find room for a little dessert.

The only good thing about the coming of the birds was that it gave Lupus and me a chance to grab an easy meal. While I kept watch over Emrys, Lupus slunk off through the underbrush and inched up close to one of the bodies. The crows flew up into the trees, squawking and protesting. It wasn't long, though, before their gluttonous desires had them settling back down. As quick as you can say Joseph of Arimathea, Lupus sprang from his hiding place and snagged himself some shiny-feathered lunch.

Lupus didn't come back until after he'd had a second helping of bird; and when he did, he looked a little sheepish, as if he knew he'd overdone it. But since we didn't know where our next meal would be coming from, I could hardly blame him for getting it while the getting was good.

Then it was my turn. I decided to try my luck at the place where the other scout had fallen, thinking those birds might not be so wary as the ones who'd just lost two of their chums. I was right. Honestly, it embarrasses me to admit how dim-witted those birds were. Maybe their brains were working slowly because they'd eaten too much. I had little difficulty in nabbing one and dragging it off into the bushes.

Later that day a few travelers finally appeared on one of the trackways leading down to the ford. None came along our little track, though, and I was beginning to realize that if Lupus and I were going to get help, we'd have to go looking for it. Emrys showed no signs of getting better. His wounds were swollen and discolored and his face was paler than I'd ever seen it. Not once did he open his eyes. Now his moans had stopped.

Lupus and I spent a second night huddled up against the body of our ailing friend. When morning came, back came the crows. They gathered around us, dark silent shapes in the trees, waiting and watching. At last a few of the bolder ones swooped down and tried to settle on our rock, but Lupus and I weren't having any of that. Yet the crows wouldn't go away. To them, Emrys was a very tempting morsel. But Lupus and I weren't about to go away either, so a standoff developed.

What finally changed things was the sound of a barking dog. It came from the trail over which Kei and his men had traveled three days earlier, the same one a few folks had used yesterday. I strained my eyes, and then through the trees I could make out an ox drawing a two-wheeled cart. A woman was walking beside it, holding a long stick, and in front of her was the barking dog.

I gave Lupus a look to let him know he should stay put, and then I dashed through the bushes so I could get ahead of the travelers. Coming out on their track maybe thirty feet below them, I lay down on the ground and placed my muzzle between my forepaws. The other dog saw me and rushed down to investigate, barking as he came. When he saw how I was lying, he slowed up and wagged his tail. He knew I wasn't there to pick a fight. He approached slowly and began sniffing me all over. I remained right where I was and let him check me out good. When he was satisfied, I stood up and took my turn at sniffing him all over.

The cart drew up in front of me and halted. The woman came toward me cautiously, studying me.

"Whatcha doin' out here all by yerself, Brownie-dog?" she said. "Maybe someone's gone and deserted ya? C'mere, then, Brownie. Let's have a look at ya."

Wiggling my hindquarters nervously and looking very sad-faced, I crept over to her. She reached out and patted my head softly. I looked up at her gratefully. Then I jumped backward three or four steps, bowed down onto my forepaws, and barked eagerly. I repeated my movements a second time.

"Whatcha ya be needin', then, Brownie?" she said. "You're wantin' to tell me somethin'? You're wantin' to show me somethin'?" You catch on quick, I thought, going through my routine once more.

"Luck," the woman said to her dog, "Stay. Stay with Oxie and the cart, Lucky-boy." Luck moved over and sat down on his haunches right in front of the ox.

Rather than leading the woman back through the bushes the way I'd come, I led her down to the ford and then up the trail to our rock on the hill. She was huffing and puffing by the time she got there, but the sight that greeted her didn't give her much time to worry about her own condition.

"Bless my soul!" she said, crossing herself. "You were wantin' to show me somethin' all right, Brownie-dog."

The woman bent over Emrys, trying to determine whether he was still alive. She put a hand on his forehead and then felt along his neck. "He's with us yet," she said, "but he's standin' on the threshold of death's dark door."

The woman went back to fetch her cart. This time Lupus tagged along while I remained with Emrys. That was when three of those greedy gluttons swooped down in a last desperate bid to get at Emrys. For one of those crows, it was his final foolish act. The other two got off easier, but they were going to be a few feathers shy of a full load for the rest of the year.

That woman was no weakling. She hauled Emrys off the rock and loaded him onto the cart all by herself. Emrys moaned softly as she handled him. Those sounds pained my heart, yet they told me my friend was hanging on to his life. The woman led us over to the other trail, and then we headed back in the direction from which she'd come. Lupus and I trotted along beside Lucky. He was the sort of dog I knew quite well—a hard-working farm dog—the sort of fellow who knew his job and did it; the sort of fellow who's a credit to dogdom.

We followed the woman for maybe three miles to a small farmstead tucked away among the hills. A tiny stone cottage sat in the middle of a clearing. Behind it was a dilapidated hen house and a dry-stone enclosure for sheep. A few chickens were scratching about in the yard. But at the sight of two strange dogs, they scittered and scattered, clucking to beat the band. Tethered to a tree near the hen house was a milk cow who gave us a blank, wide-eyed stare. In the sheep pen several black-faced sheep "baa-ed" and jostled against each other nervously.

It wasn't exactly London town, was it? No, it certainly wasn't London town. But as my master Arthur sometimes says—in a storm, any port is better than none.

VI One is the
Loneliest Number

What happened to Emrys in the days that followed I don't know. He disappeared into the cottage and we saw no more of him for quite a spell. We weren't allowed in, and Emrys was in no condition to be coming out.

Let me take a moment and tell you a little about this place where Lupus and I had landed. It was a simple, rural farmstead. Four women lived there—an old widow-woman called Mum and her daughters Janet, Margaret, and Alison. At least that's what the widow-woman called them. Amongst themselves they were Jennie, Margie, and Allie. The one who'd rescued us was Jennie, and she was the one who really ran that place.

Those four women had to work very hard just to survive. Their food was as plain as could be—mostly loaves of hard dark bread, a few eggs, and the vegetables they grew in their garden. They drank pitchers of milk fresh from their cow or else they drank water. Fortunately for us, they were quite happy to share what they had with a pair of strange dogs.

Their survival depended on their animals. Their cow and chickens provided most of what they ate and drank, but it was their sheep that gave them a means of earning money, for believe it or not, those women were in business. I guess you could call them country haberdashers, for they made and sold small items of clothing, especially scarves and gloves They spun their sheep's wool into yarn and wove the yarn into the cloth from which they made things. Warm woolen gloves was their specialty.

The day Jennie had found us she'd been on her way to a local farmer's to trade woolen goods for a fresh supply of hides. They used the hides for the leather portions of the gloves. They were clever, hard-working people, and the more I learned about their lives, the more I admired them. Of course, they didn't have a lot of time to devote to strange dogs, and at first I resented that. "You call this hospitality?" I grumped. But after a few days I realized that fussing over dogs just wasn't their way of doing things.

The one called Jennie, though, always took an interest in me. "Well, Brownie-dog," she'd say to me in the morning, "you can tag along with Luck and me, if you've a mind to." Then she'd set off on her errand, and Lucky and I would accompany her. Lupus, following some instinct I didn't share, had already found an assignment for himself—standing guard over the sheep pen. His eagerness to do that really pleased the women, who never stopped worrying about their precious sheep.

"Wolfie'll be watchin' the sheep, that he will!" Allie cried with delight—"Wolfie" was what they'd taken to calling Lupus. The very idea of a wolf volunteering to protect their sheep amused them a lot. But that's what Lupus wanted to do. He'd sit outside the sheep enclosure all day long, happily watching his little flock, being as protective and possessive as a mother hen with her chicks. Every now and then he'd jump to his feet and give them a good barking at, just to remind them who was boss. The sheep would bunch together and look at Lupus with awe-filled eyes.

Everybody on the farm had their tasks. Mum was in charge of things, but it was Jennie who looked after the farm. Margie and Allie spent their days spinning and weaving and glove-making, and as they did, they chattered away like a pair of magpies. Those two were made for softer work than Jennie, who preferred tending to the animals and the general upkeep of the farm.

It was my task to keep an eye on the chicken yard. "There's been a fox lurking about," Jennie told me, "and the thievin' devil's already helped himself to one of our hens." They could ill afford to lose any more, so I slept outside close to the hen house, keeping a sharp eye out for trouble. That was how I could "earn my keep," as Jennie put it.

I didn't much enjoy minding those chickens, but I made the best of it. The only amusement I got out of it came from the rooster in the flock, a vain little squirt who strutted all about like he was lord of the manor. The hens really adored that jaunty little cock-a-doodle, who spent most of his waking hours chasin' 'em all over, trying to get at 'em. But to my way of thinking, he was a pompous little twerp who got way too much enjoyment out of crowing his worthless head off way too early in the morning.

Lupus settled in to the routine of farm life quite readily, but I'm sorry to say I didn't. It wasn't that I didn't like those folks, I did. But I was wracked by worries—about Emrys, who'd simply disappeared into the cottage; about Arthur, who was out there somewhere in the world, facing goodness-knows what dangers; and especially about what was going to happen to Lupus and me. I missed Arthur *terribly*; I needed to know he was okay. I'd begun to fear that I might never see him again. I'd also begun to fear that Lupus and I might be spending the rest of our born days on this god-forsaken farmstead way off in the hinterlands of northern Britain.

If that sounds ungrateful, I'm sorry. If that sounds self-pitying, I'm sorry for that too. But that's how I felt. And because it was how I felt, all those feelings of fear and loneliness eventually bubbled to the surface. One night a week or so after we'd arrived there, as I was lying out under the starry skies by the hen house, I found myself giving vent to my feelings. It started out as soft little moans low in my throat. And then those moans modulated into wails. And then those wails became full-throated howls. And before I knew it, I was pouring out my soul to the heavens—

h-o-o-rooh!

h-o-o-r-o-o-h!

h-o-o-r-o-o-o-o-h-h-h!

I was raising my lonely voice in protest against the unfairness of life.

Vaguely, I heard voices from inside the cottage, voices undoubtedly telling me to shut the heck up. But I paid them no mind. Vaguely, I realized that someone had come out of the cottage and sat down beside me. Not until I felt strong, calloused hands stroking me gently did I give much heed to anything beyond my own feelings of woe. But at last I realized that Jennie was there with me, trying to soothe my anguished soul.

"Goodness, Brownie-dog," she said softly, "what a commotion you're makin'. If you keep this up, folks all over the Cheviot Hills'll be thinkin' the Prince of Wails has come a-callin'." Jennie went on stroking me and talking to me softly. Eventually her kindness began to reach me, and her concern made me feel just a teensy bit better. I licked at her hand, letting her know I appreciated her being there.

"I guess we must seem like pretty strange folks to you, Brownie-dog. I've a notion you and Wolfie are rich folks' dogs. Our way of livin' must seem pretty drab to you doggies. But we'll na treat ya bad, Brownie-dog. And when your man gets on his feet again, we'll be seein' ya safely on your way."

When my man gets on his feet again? Was Jennie telling me what I *think* she was telling me, that Emrys was getting better? Now, *that* was the best news I'd heard in a month of Sundays. I couldn't help reaching up and licking Jennie's face on hearing that, which made her laugh and push me away. "Now don'tcha be gettin' fresh, Brownie. Now don'tcha be doin' that!" But I could tell she was pleased to see me starting to perk up. And it felt good to me, too, to feel myself starting to perk up.

We sat there together, Jennnie and I, her rubbing me and stroking me, and me cosying up against her side. The stars shone brightly overhead, and it made me think of being with Arthur—sitting by the window in our little chamber back at the Red Castle, looking out at the night sky the way we used to.

"Do ya see that real bright star up there?" Jennie said, pointing almost straight overhead. "You should be knowin' *that* one, Brownie-dog," she said. "That one's *your* star." I tilted my head sideways and looked at her. *My* star? Sister, I thought, what in the world are you talking about?

"That bright one," she went on, "that one's called the Dog Star." What? The *Dog* Star? Why, I'd never heard of any *Dog* Star! *Arthur* had never told me about any *Dog* Star. *Merlin* had never told me about any *Dog* Star. *Emrys* had never told me about any *Dog* Star. And here was plain, earnest Jennie, a simple farm girl living way off in the middle of nowhere, telling me one of the most important things I'd ever heard in my whole life—that *I*, Cabal, the gentle grass-eating dog, had my own special star.

As we sat there together, close and chummie, Jennie started to hum a little tune. She hummed her way through it, and then she began putting words to it. She wasn't making them up as she went along, the way Dagonet sometimes did; but they were lovely, gentle words, though kind of sad, too. Here's what I remember.

> Oh, Brownie-dog, can love be bonnie,
>> All the while that it is new;
>> But when 'tis old it waxes cold
>> And fades away like morning dew.

> Oh, Brownie-dog, do ya see yon burn?
>> 'Tis where my love and I would go;
> There on the burnside we'd sit and talk,
>> The sweetest joy I e'er did know.
> I leaned my back against an oak,
>> I thought it was a trustie tree.
> At first it bent but then it broke—
>> And my true love grew cold to me.
> Oh, Brownie-dog, can love be bonnie,
>> All the while that it is new;
>> But when 'tis old it waxes cold
>> And fades away like morning dew.

> So why should I care to trim my cap,
>> And why should I comb my hair?
> My own true love has forsaken me
> And now no more will meet me there.
> Had I but known before I kissed

That true love was so hard to win,
I'd've placed my heart in a case of gold
And locked it tight with a silver pin.

Oh, Brownie-dog, can love be bonnie,
All the while that it is new;
But when 'tis old it waxes cold
And fades away like morning dew.

Every night after that, Jennie would come and sit beside me and sing to me. And all her songs were love songs—and they were the saddest love songs I'd ever heard.

VII When the Fox Preaches,
Look after your Geese!

Do you remember the night we tore through the Northgalian camp, trying to reach the safety of Carmelide—the night my poor brother got bashed and battered by some stinking Northgalian soldiers? If you do, then you probably remember that a very strange thing happened to me that night. For the first time that night I'd begun experiencing the very same feelings my brother was experiencing. Believe me, it was terribly frightening and confusing. And following that night, whenever my brother was under a great deal of emotional stress, his feelings would pop up right inside my head, just like it was the most natural thing in the world. Believe me, this business of sharing my brother's feelings took quite a bit of getting used to. That first night it happened, it turned out to be really important for the both of us. Later on, it turned out to be really important for every living soul in Britain.

Having my brother's feelings communicated to me like that, I realized, was kind of like what happens when Merlin sends a message right straight inside my little dog brain. There I am, going along just minding my own business, when out of nowhere a message from Merlin comes flashing into my head. Of course when Merlin sends me a message, he's doing it on purpose. Lupus, I'm pretty sure, doesn't realize that he's sharing his most powerful feelings with me. If he did, I doubt if he'd like it very much.

Anyway, a couple of weeks after we arrived at Jenny's farm, I was lying out under the stars one night, more or less attending to my job, which was to keep an eye on the hen house. And as I lay there, not quite asleep and not quite awake, I began to hear an odd little voice speaking right inside my head—just the way Merlin's voice sometimes does—though this time it certainly wasn't Merlin. My first thought was that I had to be dreaming. I *wasn't*.

"Got those cobwebs cleared away yet, cousin?" said the voice. "Come on, now, let me see if you're really the very bright boy I've taken you to be."

I got to my feet and looked all around. If somebody was out there playing games with me, I knew they had to be close by. Even Merlin can't send his messages over very great distances. I looked and stared and peered, but without success. The sad truth is that my nighttime vision isn't any great shakes. As I'm sure you'll agree, dogs are superior to cats in just about every way; still, when it comes to seeing in the dark, my honor forces me to admit that in this one thing those sleek-furred felines have the advantage over their canine betters.

"Can't see me, cousin? Can't quite lay your eyes upon me? Do you think perhaps that I don't really exist? Do you think I'm just a figment of your imagination? Let me assure you that I'm *not*. I'm as real as you are. And you're as real as me. We're two of a kind, really, and the fact that you can hear me at all, and the fact that I can hear you in return— maybe you didn't know that, but I can—just goes to show you how closely connected the two of us are. We're two of a kind, cousin, and it's our superior intelligence that connects us."

Have I gone *wacko*, I wondered? Have my worries about Emrys and Arthur and about what's going to happen to Lupus and me caused me to go completely 'round the bend?

"Now, don't be fretting yourself, cousin," said the voice. "Believe me, I really am talking to you. You're no more wacko than I am."

My word, I thought, this is just like having a mental conversation with Merlin—only *more so*.

"Congratulations, cousin. I'm proud of you. You've figured things out. Believe me, it's a rare dog who can do that. Most of your kind, I'm sorry to say, have become an embarrassment to our species. Like your wolfish companion who's sleeping out by the sheep pen. I'm sure he must have his good points, but honestly, that fellow's as thick as a brick. I tried communicating with him a couple of times just last night without the least bit of success. And he looked rather promising, too. A shame, really. But *you*, my friend, are another matter altogether. *You*, I can see, are a worthy compatriot. And it's a pleasure to make your acquaintance."

Once more I looked all about me, trying to locate the source of this haughty little voice that had intruded itself into my head. And at last I *did*. There, staring out of a clump of laurels maybe thirty yards up the hill, were a pair of red glowing coals—the eyes of a creature burning brightly in the night. At that point I cranked up my nose to its highest degree of smellability and sniffed the air for all I was worth—and then I knew for sure. Yes, it was *Foxie*, the very fellow Jennie had told me to watch out for.

"Spotted me at last, have you? Well done, my sharp-eyed, sharp-nosed friend, well done indeed. I must say, you really are a splendid chap. Smart, quick, alert—excellent qualities in a watchdog of your sort. Qualities that are sadly lacking in most. But I can tell that you are a very special fellow, cousin, indeed you are. Still, I can't help thinking it's a terrible shame that someone with such sterling qualities would so willingly debase himself. Now, why would you go and do that, cousin, a sterling fellow like you? Such a pity."

"Wait a second," I said, beginning to take umbrage at the rudeness of this haughty fellow. "What do you mean *debase* myself?"

"Well, cousin," the sharp little voice came back, "take a look at yourself. Look at all your God-given talents. Look at all your unusual abilities. And then take a good look at your situation. There you are—there *you* are, a dog with such marvelous gifts—and what are you doing? Lying there like some pathetic lackey, carrying out boring, menial chores, waiting for whatever handouts—pitiful charity, really—might be coming your way. Don't you think that's *debasing* your-self?"

I wasn't too happy with the way this conversation was going. This Foxie was a very smart fellow all right, there was no getting around that, and he had quite a way with words. Still, a lot of the things he was saying were downright insult-ing and I'd about had my fill of it.

"Listen to *me*, wise guy," I said within my head, "how about you keep your insults to yourself. If you don't like my way of life, that's okay with me. The truth is, you don't know anything about me, and I don't know anything about you. If you want to get acquainted, fine. But lay off with the in-sults."

"Oh, my fine young friend, don't be so prickly. All I'm doing is pointing out a very simple fact. There you are, watching and waking all night long, working very hard at guarding that paltry bunch of brainless chickens. And for what? A bit of breakfast slops? It hardly seems worth it, does it? You do all the work and they keep all the eggs. They get all the good stuff and you get all the leftovers. I wouldn't call *that* fair, would you?"

There was a pause before he continued. "Allow me to make a suggestion. Why don't you and I—we really are two of a kind, you know—why don't you and I simply join forces. Two bright fellows like us, we could have ourselves a pretty fine time of it. What you and I could do, if you've a mind to, is divide up all those chickens and enjoy them our-selves. Wouldn't that beat a breakfast of leftover slops? I think it would, my fine, intelligent friend, I think it would. Yes, that would be a meal worthy of a person of your talents."

The more this clever bugger talked, the madder I got. Foxie was proposing that I should turn against my friends and become a lawless renegade. I've *known* a few dogs that've done that, dogs who returned to the wild and had to roam and forage and live an outlaw's life; they were miserable, pathetic creatures, and I wanted no part of any such life. Besides, I had pledged my word to Jennie that I would protect her chickens, and she was counting on me. Was I going to go back on my pledge? What would my master Arthur think if he knew I'd gone back on a sacred pledge?

No, this Foxie fellow hadn't fooled me one bit. He was nothing but a liar, a sneak, and a thief. He was working very hard at appealing to my baser instincts, baser instincts he darn well knew I had. He was trying to turn me against all that I believed was right. But that was *not* going to happen. No, it was high time for me to get rid of this wily, wicked tempter.

"Cousin," I said inside my head, "I'm ashamed to admit how slow I've been to see the wisdom in your words. Honestly, sharing a delicious chicken dinner with you is quite an appealing prospect. Why don't you come on down here and join me, cousin, and then the two of us can get on with it. But I hope you'll allow me the privilege of biting the head off of that silly rooster—I've been itching to get my paws on that pompous little twerp ever since I got here."

My words of invitation were greeted by a long silence. Foxie must've been weighing them carefully. "C'mon down," I said again. "The idea of that chicken dinner has got my digestive juices flowing to beat the band. You can have the first pick of the hens, just let me have the rooster. Come on down, cousin. Let's us have ourselves a moonlight banquet."

But the wily fox wasn't fooled by my sudden change of heart. Either that, or he was able to read my deepest thoughts, which I was doing my best to conceal.

"Cousin," he said at last, "the hour is late, and I've just remembered some pressing business I must attend to on the far side of the ridge. It's been a pleasure talking with you, and I look forward to having another chat with you some time soon. At the moment, though, I must bid you a fond adieu." And then Foxie's bright eyes disappeared from the laurel clump, and his foxy-ish smell receded up the slope and faded away in the night air.

VIII   The Wonder of
New-Found Joy

One morning a few days after my encounter with the fox, Jennie came barging out of the cottage. She was grinning from ear to ear and seemed terribly excited.

"C'mon, you dogs!" she exclaimed cheerfully. "C'mon and be eatin' up. There's things that need a-doin'."

At breakfast time around there it was every dog for himself, and those who were slow of paw or jaw were likely to be missing out. So the three of us stood there muzzle to muzzle to muzzle, gobbling down a sloppy mess of bread crusts soaked in milk. I kept one eye on my food, of course, but the other I kept on Jennie, wondering what had gotten into her. She was humming away like a buzzy bumblebee on a bright May morning.

"C'mon, then, Brownie-dog," she said, "you can be comin' along. Wolfie and Lucky, you can be keepin' an eye on things. Brownie-dog, you and me have things to be doin'."

Then she was off, moving in those huge ungainly strides of hers, lurching up the slope behind the hen house. I bounded after her, curious as anything to know what in the world she was up to.

Soon she was thrashing about in the underbrush, her eyes darting this way and that. "Here we are, then," she said at last. "Emrys'll be needing a bit of *this*." She snapped a sprig off of a flowering shrub and popped it into the wicker basket she had over her arm. "And he's a-wantin' some of *this*, too," she said, stripping a whole row of leaves off a small branch.

During the next hour Jennie scurried all over that hillside grabbing up bits of flowers, leaves, berries, and bark. I even helped her dig up a few roots. I didn't understand what was going on, but Jennie was clearly a woman on a mission. But finally my little dog brain began to sort things out. Emrys had *told* her to collect this stuff. Emrys was *talking*! Emrys was *awake* and *talking*—and realizing that, I jumped for joy. Now Jennie wasn't the only one capering about on that hillside.

When we got back to the cottage, Jennie took her basket of treasures straight inside, and I barged in right behind her. I knew I wasn't supposed to, but I couldn't help it.

"Hey, you old Brown-dog!" came a stern voice out of the corner of the room. "You mustn't be in here!"

It was Mum, the old widow-woman, and she sounded irked. But I *had* to see Emrys. I *had* to see him, and there he was—lying on his side, looking right at me. His face was drawn and pale, but there was a smile in his eyes. I could tell he was badly in need of a face-licking, which I promptly administered. Emrys reached out to pat me, and the effort caused him to wince with pain.

"Cabal," he murmured, "your furry old face is a lovely sight to see. I've missed you, dog. But the good Lord willing, you and me'll be tussling in the leaves before much longer."

Emrys and I *wouldn't* be tussling in the leaves any time soon, I was sure of that. Still, he was on his way back to us—back from death's dark door—and that's why I was shaking all over with joy.

"*Now, Janet!*" came the old woman's voice again. "You be gettin' that ill-mannered creature out of here, d'ya hear me? Why, look at him. He's slobberin' on the counterpane." As stern as the old woman's voice sounded, I detected a hint of warmth. She knew how much I needed to see Emrys and how much Emrys needed to see me. Jennie took hold of my collar and shooed me out the door, but I didn't mind her rough handling. Emrys was on the mend, and nothing else mattered.

That was my happiest day at the farmstead. All day long I went about my business with a cheerful little tune bouncing around inside my heart:

"Emrys is getting better;

Who could ask for jollier weather?

Purpling now is the heather;

Kei and Arthur are safely together."

If I'd been Taliesin, I would've shared my happy little tune with the world. But we both know what happens when dogs try to sing. So I kept my song to myself, safely tucked away inside my heart.

As I lay out under the starry skies that night, Jennie came out as usual to sit with me and sing to me. That night she didn't sing about the sadness of love that doesn't last. She sang about the rebirth of nature in the springtime, and about the joy and hope of love when it's new. Now, what had gotten into this lass? What had caused her so suddenly to change her tune? Then I remembered what had caused me to change my tune—*Emrys*. Maybe Emrys was causing Jennie to change her tune, too. Maybe Emrys was the cause of Jennie's new-found joy.

One morning a few days later Emrys appeared in the cottage doorway. He stood propped up by Jennie and Allie, and he resembled a weak damp butterfly emerging from its cocoon. With an arm around each woman's shoulders, Emrys shuffled slowly out into the morning light, the effort showing in his face. He was still a long way from being his old self again, but now he was nowhere near to death's dark door. Emrys was firmly in the land of the living.

I really couldn't say how long it'd been since Emrys had disappeared inside the cottage. But while he'd been in there the season of summer hadn't stood still. Just the other night as Jennie and I were sitting beneath the starry sky, she said that we were now in the Dog Days. I cocked my head questioningly—the Dog Days? Jennie said they lasted for a few weeks late in the summer, when the Dog Star stays close to the sun. I wondered if Jennie was pulling my leg, but somehow I doubted it. Leg-pulling wasn't her style.

That morning Emrys sat outside for at least an hour, soaking up the late summer sun. It felt good to be sitting there like that, with Jennie on one side of him and me on the other. This was one of the only times I'd ever seen Jennie take a break from her chores. Lazing about on a summer's morn wasn't at all like her. Allie and Margie would have idle hands once in a while, but never Jennie. It must've been important to her to sit there with Emrys and me. Maybe she knew this would be one of the only times she'd be able to do that.

Later that day an unexpected visitor showed up. Lucky spotted him as he strode quickly over the hill and down the path toward the cottage. Lucky charged out and confronted the fellow, but then he began to wag his tail and bark cheerfully. Our visitor was no stranger to Lucky, but he was to me, and these days one can't be too careful. So I dashed out to do my own investigating. As I sniffed him over good he stood there calmly smiling. Scenting no danger, I decided to go along with Lucky's assessment—at least for the time being.

He was a wizened little fella, so short that his walking stick rose above his nearly-bald head. He wore a coarse gray robe tied about his round tummy by a rope. His face looked like a dried-up apple, and astonishingly, he was *clean-shaven*. It's very unusual to see an older fellow without a beard, and when you do, it's pretty creepy. But the fellow seemed innocent enough, and his brown eyes sparkled with amusement.

When he saw that he'd met my approval, his face broke into a grin, revealing a mouth chockfull of pointy little teeth.

"Brother John!" Jennie sang out from behind me. "You be mickle welcome, Brother John!" Charging over to him, she wrapped her strong arms around him and hugged him to her chest. She seemed to be crushing the little fellow, who just stood there grinning, his round bald head tucked neatly beneath Jenny's chin. When she finally released him, Brother John nodded his head in my direction and said, "Who's *this* bright-eyed fellow, then, Jennie-girl? Luck's got someone new to lend him a paw with the chores?"

"He's got a pair of 'em," Jennie replied. "This here Brownie-dog, I'm now a-knowin', is called Cabal. And his brother Lupus is up yonder, watching the woolies."

Hardly having to stoop because he was so short, Brother John placed his hands behind my ears and scratched me vigorously. Then he rubbed me back and forth on my sides before slapping me firmly, causing me to say "oof!" "*Cabal* and *Lupus*, you say? Why, Jennie-girl, I b'lieve I've heard of these two fellas. Now, ya don't be tellin' me that Arthur and Kei are hereabouts as well?"

"There isna any Arthur or Kei," Jennie said, "but there's a bonnie lad in charge of them whose name is Emrys. He's been bad hurt, Brother John, but he's mickle better just lately. Do ya be knowin' Emrys and the doggies, then?"

"Aye, Jennie-lass, in a way I do. I'd not actually seen them till now, but I've heard about them often enough. Your Emrys must be Merlin's new lad. As for the dogs, I'm fairly certain they belong to King Arthur and his brother, the royal seneschal Sir Kei. It appears that you've been keepin' some mighty fine company, Jennie-girl."

Jennie just stood there all a-gawk. "Brother John," she managed at last, "are ya sayin' you were thinkin' the High King of Britain and his brother might be *here*? Are ya tellin' me *that*, Brother John?"

"Aye, Jennie-lass, that's the thought that was crossin' my mind."

That evening we sat down to the finest meal the widow-woman and her daughters could put together. As far as us dogs were concerned, the highlights of the meal were bread crusts smothered in mutton gravy and then the mutton bones themselves. Each of us dragged one off to a private place where we could gnaw away to our heart's content. After supper the entire group of us—except for Lupus, who went back to guarding the woolies—set off for the top of the hill, aiming for a grassy spot where Brother John could lead us in evening devotions.

Brother John, I now knew, was a friar. Not only was he a friar, but he belonged to the very same friary that Emrys and Lupus and I were seeking. He worked with Brother Blaise, Merlin's friend and teacher, and he knew Merlin quite well. He'd even met Arthur and Kei. That was a few years ago when Merlin had whisked them away from the Red Castle for safekeeping. I remembered that time very well, for it was the first time Arthur and I had ever been away from each other.

It was a glorious summer evening in the Cheviot Hills. The sounds of the cuckoos echoed through the vales and dales. The day's warmth was past now, and it would turn chilly later, but now the air was fresh and cool. The clouds in the western sky were streaked with pink and orange. There on the grassy slope we found comfortable spots to sit while we listened to Brother John. Jennie helped Emrys ease down on the grass where he could lean back against a tree. Then she plopped down beside him and snuggled up against his unin-jured shoulder.

Brother John stood there before us, beaming his toothy little grin. Then he closed his eyes and began to recite: "*Coeli enarrant gloriam Dei, et opera manuum ejus annunciat firmamentum.*" Maybe Emrys could understand his jibberish but the rest of us sure couldn't! And then he began to sing in a low firm voice:

> The heavens proclaim the glory of the Lord,
> The skies declare His wonders—
> Every day and every night,
> In sunshine, rain, or thunder.
> Creation makes no sound or noise
> Wherein the Lord's voice isn't heard:
> In all the lands that fill the world,
> Nature proclaims God's holy word.
> All lovely forms declare His love,
> Creation speaks His praise;
> And every thing—above, below—
> With faith His will obeys.

Established is His perfect law,
    And perfect shall it stand,
Imprinted in each creature's heart—
    In sea, in air, on land.

part III

"For auld lang syne, my dear,
For auld lang syne,
We'll take a cup o' kindness yet
For auld lang syne."

— *Robert Burns*

I   *In Malachi's Cave*

He isna ready, Brother John, he *isna*! He's mickle better, aye, but he isna ready to be *travelin'*, Brother John!"

"Jennie-lass, Jennie-lass, now don't be frettin' yourself. He's a-*wantin'* to go and he's a-*needin'* to go. I'll be by his side every step of the way to Crastor. It be no more than twenty-five or thirty miles, Jennie. No harm'll be coming to our Emrys, I can promise ya that."

Jennie took a great deal of persuading, but being the practical girl she was, she finally accepted the fact that we were leaving. When she did, tears filled her eyes. And she wasn't alone in that, for Lupus and Emrys and I felt some real sadness at saying goodbye to these good-hearted folks who'd taken us in and treated us so kindly.

For the first time in weeks Emrys' horse Pwyll was saddled, and now Brother John stood beside him, holding the reins, waiting for Emrys to mount. Lupus and I made a final run around the farmstead, barking our farewells to the animals we'd come to know there. Then we were ready to be off, ready to finish the journey that would lead us to Brother Blaise, and just maybe, to Kei and Arthur.

As Emrys was preparing to mount up, Jennie came over and wrapped her arms around him, resting her head against his good shoulder. Reluctantly she let go and stepped back. Smiling at her, Emrys put his hand inside his tunic and pulled out a leather pouch that was hanging around his neck. Inside that pouch, I knew, was Emrys' pride and joy. It was an amulet, a very special good luck charm that he was never without.

"Would you be takin' care of this for me, Jennie-girl?" he asked her softly. My word, was I ever surprised at that. "Would you be keeping it for me? If you will, then I'll hafta be coming back here to see how much luck it's brought you."

Jennie took the pouch from Emrys. She loosened the drawstring and lifted out a small blue stone. I didn't need Melleas to tell me that it was lapis lazuli. I'd heard Merlin say that someone he knew had brought it all the way from a place called Araby; and if Merlin had said it, it was probably true. But the only thing *I* knew for sure about that lovely little stone was that it meant a great deal to Emrys.

Jennie looked at the stone in wonder, and then her eyes went back to Emrys' face. Now she was smiling through her tears, for now she knew that Emrys would be coming back to see her. Well, lass, I said to myself, any dumb bunny could have told you *that*.

We traveled slowly that day, stopping often. Brother John wasn't taking any chances with Emrys not being up to the journey. As late afternoon faded into evening, we found ourselves on a path beside a small river. The skies were sullen and the weather was closing in. Soon we were slipping and slopping along the muddy path, getting thoroughly soaked by a steady drizzle. The bushes lining the path were wet and cold and I tried my best to avoid brushing against them. Before long my poor little paddy-paws were clogged with mud.

As we rounded a bend in the river, I saw up ahead of us a set of crude steps carved right into the embankment. "Ah," said Brother John, "here we are at last. This is what I've been looking for."

We followed him up the steps to a dark gaping hole in the earthen wall. There we halted, peering into the gloom. Goodness, what kind of a place *is* this? I was afraid it might be the entrance to the lair of some terrible monster or a den where bears hide out in winter. Or maybe, I thought, letting my imagination run away with me, it was the gateway to the Land of Faerie, a magical and mysterious Otherworld I'd heard Taliesin sing about. As those possibilities rushed through my mind, I was completely convinced we should find some *other* place to spend the night.

We heard rustling sounds from within, and my nose was twitching to some very peculiar odors. I tensed my muscles, preparing for the worst. And then one of the oldest faces I'd ever seen materialized before us in that dark entranceway.

"Why, Brother John!" said a dry raspy voice that sounded like it needed a good oiling, "ye be mickle welcome, Brother John. *All* of ye be mickle welcome."

The raspy voice didn't belong to an ogre or a wood elf—or even to a bear! It belonged to a man who looked truly ancient. His name was Malachi, but it seemed to me it should've been Methuselah. Anyway, he was what folks call a hermit, a kind of religious fellow who lives all by himself and devotes all his time to thinking and writing and praying.

I had no objection to how this old fellow chose to live his life; that was *his* business. But my word, what a strange place he'd chosen to live in. For the life of me, I couldn't understand why anyone would choose to creep about all day in a dark dank mole-hole! But Malachi was a kindly old fellow, and he welcomed us warmly and did all he could to make us comfortable. He lit some tallow candles that were stuck into various cracks and crevices along the walls of the cave and threw a few pieces of wood onto his fire. It wasn't long before that mole-hole of his began to seem a lot less dreary.

Lupus and I wasted no time in checking the place out good. We were pleased to discover that the cave had a dry sandy floor and that little bunches of aromatic herbs placed here and there bestowed upon it a refreshing fragrance. No, that cave wasn't at all the damp and musty mole-hole I'd thought it would be.

Along the walls Malachi had scraped several shelves right out of the rock; they were all a-jumble with books and parchments and other odds and ends I couldn't identify. Near the back of the cave was a smaller room mostly taken up by an altar formed from large stones; high up in the altar room was an opening that let in air and light. This is the hermit's special sanctuary, I thought, the place where he keeps his private devotions.

"Draw thee up close to the fire," Malachi croaked softly to us after we'd finished our investigations, "for the night be thickenin'." We flopped ourselves down comfortably on the sand. By then the warmth from the fire had spread through the cave making that strange dark place feel almost cozy.

Emrys and Brother John reached into their knapsacks and brought out hunks of bread and cheese. They offered the food to Malachi but the old hermit declined their offer. He got his only nourishment from some thick soup which at that very moment was simmering in a blackened pot hanging from a tripod over his fire. But while Malachi didn't choose to partake of our food, we weren't shy about partaking of his, and his soup turned out to be the perfect complement to our bread and cheese. It was thick and savory and filled with carrots and onions and some root-like things I couldn't identify. It had a salty taste that took a bit of getting used to; but after I'd licked my bowl clean I didn't turn down the offer of seconds—or even of thirds.

I was still uneasy about spending the night in the hermit's subterranean abode, but my worries were groundless. With that warm nourishing supper in my belly and my fur thoroughly dried by the warmth of the fire, I lay down contentedly on the sandy floor of the cave and quickly fell asleep. Sometime later in the night I felt a very great need to be going outside. Perhaps my several helpings of Malachi's soup had something to do with it. I padded out of the cave as silently as I could so as not to disturb the others.

After I'd taken care of my urgent needs, I stood quietly alone in the dark beside the entrance to the cave and treated myself to several big lungfuls of the refreshing night air. The light rain we'd traveled through that day was gone now, and overhead the stars were shining brightly. Off in the west just above the horizon I could see the Dog Star Jennie had told me about. And spreading all across the sky overhead was the bright band of stars Arthur called Watling Street. They reminded me of those nights long ago when Arthur and I would look out at the stars from our little chamber in the Red Castle, back when we were both young pups.

But when, oh when would I ever see *Arthur* again? I didn't know how long it had been since I'd last seen him. Emrys was a wonderful friend, and I cared about him dearly. And Jennie had been very, very kind to me; she would always have a special place in my heart. But as much as I loved them, the truth of the matter is that they weren't Arthur. There was only *one* Arthur. I missed him *terribly*. I needed to know that he was okay.

And then a startling thought popped up inside my head. Right at that moment I felt certain that Arthur was doing exactly what I was doing. Arthur was out there somewhere in the dark and he was looking up at the starry night sky. My master Arthur was thinking and feeling the very same things that I was thinking and feeling. I felt certain of it! And then

I knew in my heart that Arthur *was* okay. And I had a very strong feeling it wouldn't be long before I would see him again.

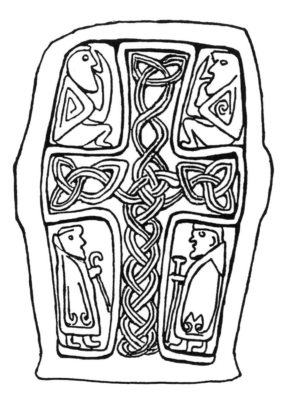

II   The Devil

& the Deep Blue Sea

"It won't be long now," Brother John told us the next morning after we'd bid farewell to Malachi. "If nothing untoward happens today, we should reach the friary 'round about supper time."

Those were magical words to me— "it won't be long now"—and they caused a little tune to burble up inside my heart:

> "If we don't dawdle or too long abide,
> We'll be there by eventide."

There was where Blaise was, and *there*, just maybe, was where Arthur was. Then I considered the other thing Brother John had said— "if nothing *untoward* happens today." I wasn't sure what "untoward" meant, but I had a pretty good idea. As long as we didn't have any unexpected surprises, we should get there by this evening. But wouldn't you know it—something untoward *did* happen that day!

By early afternoon we'd passed out of the wooded hills and were following a little trail that took us across open moorland. Clumps of rocks poked up here and there, along with scattterings of scrubby trees, but that rolling moor was mostly carpeted with wildflowers, heather, and gorse. And then I began to notice a very different smell in the air, a kind of tangy, salty smell. It reminded me of a smell I'd first encountered along the River Thames in London town.

As we came over a rise in the trail, we were greeted by an astonishing sight—in between where the moorland dropped down low and the clouds rose up high was nothing but a huge expanse of grayness. I stopped right in my tracks and stared at it. I didn't know what in the world it could be. I looked at Emrys and I looked at Brother John, and then I looked back at that great gray vastness.

"We're right close now," Brother John said. "Now we can angle on over to the coastal path and head straight on north to Crastor. It won't be long now, lads," he said, grinning his toothy grin, "it won't be long now." Brother John was as anxious to get there as the rest of us were.

By now you've probably guessed what it was I'd been smelling and seeing—it was the *sea*! Believe me, it was like nothing I had ever seen before. If you've never seen the sea, then you can't imagine it either, for there isn't anything else like it. It's huge and wet and cold; it's noisy and constantly moving; and it's filled with a symphony of very strange smells. But we didn't have much chance to be contemplating the sea, for that's when the "untoward" thing Brother John had warned us about happened—and it was something that required our full attention.

Just after we'd come over the rise where we had our first glimpse of the sea, we heard a great commotion off to our right. A lone horseman came crashing through a clump of those scrubby little trees. He was riding like all get-out and we soon knew why. Not far behind another fellow was giving chase, a huge and fearsome fellow who was mounted on a very swift courser. In his right arm he griped a gigantic battle-ax which he intended to use on the first fellow. Just as he was closing in, that second fellow became the object of a swift and unexpected attack

Out of nowhere came a long silver dog. In the first blink of an eye he caught up with the man with the battle-ax, and in the next blink of an eye he knocked that fellow right out of his saddle and into a prickly clump of bracken. And then we became aware of yet *another* rider! This third fellow, who was all decked out in knightly finery, came dashing along on a splendid white stallion. He gave a loud whistle, and the long silver dog immediately left off tearing at the fallen man's sleeve and went bounding after his master.

In no time at all the knight and his dog had caught up with the first rider, who was obviously their friend; but it was right at that point that a whole troop of riders came galloping across the moor. These fellows were dressed like the guy who'd been knocked off his horse, and it didn't take a genius to know they were his companions. In the very next moment the whole bunch of them came charging right in our direction.

"It's *Tristrem!*" cried Brother John, "and he's in a jam. Quick! Into this thicket or we'll be in it too!" But it was too late for that, for the first two men and the long silver dog were practically on top of us, and that large troop of rough-looking riders was headed straight for us.

"Up on my horse, Brother friar!" the man named Tristrem shouted. "Quick! We've got to run for it." He grabbed Brother John's arm and swung him up behind him. "Come on!" he yelled at Emrys. "Ride or perish!"

Emrys dug his spurs into Pwyll's sides, and Lupus and I dug our paws into the loose sandy soil. We tore across the moor with the riders coming hard behind us. After our long stay at Jennie's farm I felt fit and well rested, and despite the fact that we were running for our lives, it felt good to be pushing my body to the limit. I'm Cabal le Savage, I barked out, and if you think you can capture me you're even dumber than you look!

As we made our run for safety, every one of us was keeping up a very fast pace—perhaps because we were as fit as a fiddle or perhaps because we were as scared as heck! But who cares, right? The important thing was that we were all doing very well. But as well as the rest of us were doing, it was nothing compared to how well Tristrem's long silvery dog was doing, for that lean lanky fellow was putting on a dazzling display of athleticism.

Tristrem's dog—whose name was Wisp—was the fastest four-legged creature I'd ever laid eyes on. I've known some pretty swift mutts in my time but not a one of 'em could hold a candle to Wisp; that fellow belonged at the very top of the list. Tristrem's mount was excellent too, which was a good thing, considering the fact that he had to bear the weight of both Tristrem and Brother John. Emrys and Pwyll, I was relieved to see, were holding up their end of things just fine also.

Finally our haven of refuge hoved into view—a gleaming white castle on a strip of land sticking out into the sea. We followed Wisp across a little bridge and onto the castle foreground, an open field enclosed on both sides by the sea. Behind us we heard the hooves of our pursuers' horses as they clattered across the wooden bridge—so close it seemed they'd be on us before we could get inside the castle.

The doors of the castle flew open and riders poured out. They came right at us. For a moment I thought Wisp had led us into a trap. But they were Tristrem's men, and they intended to do battle with those brutes who'd been breathing down our necks. We swerved out of their way and skidded to a halt beside the castle moat; then panting and sweating, we turned to watch the combat that was about to commence.

"Who *are* those fellows, Tristrem?" said Brother John, wiping sweat off his brow.

"Danish mercenaries, Brother John, brought over by King Nentres. He's been using them to guard the border with Scotland. But as you can plainly see, *they've* become a bigger menace than the blasted Scots!"

Out on the castle foreground the two groups of warriors maneuvered about, each trying to arrange themselves to best advantage; but before they could tangle, another group of riders came charging across the bridge. *These* were fellows I was very happy to see—for I knew in a flash they were *Arthur's* men! I ran my eyes over them quickly, hoping and praying to see Arthur and Tawnyfoot. I looked and looked and hoped and hoped, but they weren't there!

I recognized several of the horses—Goldenrod, Sir Bedivere's shinning charger; Valencia, Sir Lucan's tall bay stallion; and Moloch, Sir Griflet's massive warhorse. Riding close beside those famous knights were two much smaller figures. One was Dagonet, the little minstrel-knight; but I didn't have the foggiest notion who the other might be. He was a tiny little fellow who looked more like a lad than a man—but as his actions would soon reveal, he was hardly any lad.

Arthur's men swooped down upon the Danes from the rear while the fellows from the castle attacked them from the front. Those blasted Danes now found themselves neatly trapped between the devil and the deep blue sea. They knew it, too, but that didn't stop them from putting up a very stiff fight. They were powerful fellows who fought with reckless abandon. Their horsemanship was pathetic, but their ferocity helped to offset their other deficiencies. They crashed and bashed and thrashed, taking mighty swipes with their clubs and axes. They fought more like rampaging bulls than like noble warriors, but rampaging bulls can inflict a whole lot of hurt.

As the fight went on, the Danes were gradually being whittled down. And the fellow who was doing a lot of the whittling was the little man riding next to Dagonet. His pony didn't even have a saddle, but he guided it skillfully with his knees and his right hand which was twisted in its mane. He wore no armor and carried no sword, but crisscrossing his chest were two broad belts and each one was jam-packed with knives. As he rode about on the battlefield, dodging and ducking the Danes' hefty blows, he kept up a steady process of plucking a knife out of a belt—with his *teeth*, no less! Holding the tip between his fingers, he'd flick the wrist of his hand. The next thing you knew that knife was buried in the throat of one of those dastardly Danes! Holy cats, I thought, will wonders never cease.

When only a handful of Danes were still mounted, their leader decided it was time to call it quits. This fellow, who was the hugest of them all—we learned later he was called Osla Big Knife—barked out a command, and then those last few fellows tossed down their weapons, tumbled off their mounts, and threw themselves on Sir Bedivere's mercy.

"*No mercy*," I barked, "*no dad-blasted mercy*! How much mercy would they show us if *they'd* won?"

Tristrem looked at me and laughed. "If your dog is saying what I think he's saying," he said, "he's entirely right. Now watch. The next thing the Danes will do is try to get *us* to hire them to fight against Nentres and Angus. That's the way these noble fellows operate."

Emrys looked startled. "What did you just say? Nentres has taken up with Angus? Nentres is now standing in open opposition to Arthur?"

Tristrem gave Emrys a wide-eyed stare. "Where in the world have *you* been, my friend? It's plain to see you have some catching up to do. Come along then, and we'll get you up to date over a mug of ale and a steaming chop of venison." A steaming chop of venison!—I barked out to nobody in particular. Tristrem, my friend, now you're talking!

With a sweep of his arm Tristrem said, "Welcome, my new-found friends, to the Castle of Joyous Garde."

III A Sure Cure for the Blues

My feelings that night were completely jumbled up. I knew we were safe, in the company of good friends, and close to our final destination. Yet I couldn't shake off an overwhelming sense of sadness. Where, oh where, I wondered, was my master Arthur? When would I see him again? I'd even begun to wonder if I would *ever* see him again.

One of the causes for my blues was Joyous Garde itself, Tristrem's magnificent castle. Over the last few months we stayed in some pretty primitive places—sometimes in the open countryside, sometimes in forest campsites, sometimes in barns, sometimes in plain and simple farmsteads, and once we even stayed in a cave. Tristrem's lovely, comfortable castle was a welcome and refreshing change, but it reminded me far too much of the place where Arthur and I had grown up. Of course Joyous Garde, with its gleaming white walls, was much grander than the damp and drafty old Red Castle. But as I stood there admiring the soaring towers and the cobblestone courtyard, the great hall and the many-stalled stables, I couldn't help thinking of home. All those things reminded me once more how terribly much I missed Arthur, the kindest master any dog has ever had.

I honestly tried my best to buck up that evening. After all, Tristrem was being a generous and gracious host. It also helped being surrounded by a host of friends—Emrys and Brother John; Sir Bedivere, Sir Lucan and Sir Griflet; and my inspiring new friend Wisp the wonder dog. Dagonet was there too, along with the little chap who'd put on such an amazing display of knife throwing during the battle.

Dagonet's friend was called Gwythir, and I learned that he was one of the last surviving Picts. The Picts, in case you don't know, are a race of small folks who used to live all over the north of Britain. Then the blasted Scots came to Britain from Ireland and drove the Picts right out of their own land. Now just a few scattered bands of Picts were all that remained. I think you can understand why Gwythir had no great love for the Scots.

Gwythir had a high twittery voice, and his words sounded kind of funny. That was because he normally spoke a language that was very different from ours. But as a matter of fact, it turned out that Gwythir was able to speak a *cartload* of different languages. The little fellow had a knack for learning them, and that's why later on he became known at Arthur's court as Gwythir the Interpreter. Nyneve once called Gwythir a walking, talking Tower of Babel. When Kei heard that he just laughed and said, "Maybe so, but a rather *pint-sized* Tower of Babel, wouldn't you say?"

The best way to escape my blues, I found, was to focus all my attention on the conversations going on around me; I paid particularly close attention to what Tristrem was telling Emrys. That's how I learned what'd happened to Arthur while we'd been at Jennie's farm. It turned out that King Nentres really had been trying to trap Arthur—just as Emrys had suspected—but wily old Arthur fooled Nentres completely. While Nentres' war parties were out chasing after Kei's troop, Arthur snuck up and made a surprise attack on his castle.

Before daybreak Arthur's men burst right into Nentres' stronghold, capturing his main force without a fight. Unfortunately, Nentres and his chief advisors escaped. They fled north to Scotland and took shelter with King Angus. The rest of Nentres' men, not being total fools, quickly swore their fealty to Arthur, and now they'd been added to Arthur's army.

Kei and his men were the ones who'd been involved in the greatest amount of action. As they were leaving Durham Nentres' scouts had spotted them, and in the days that followed they engaged Kei's troop in several running battles. It was one of those in which Emrys was injured. Kei and his men had had a rough time of it, but in the end they'd come through all their trials and tribulations in fairly decent shape.

Tristrem also told us that Arthur had offered King Angus a deal—if the Scots would agree to stay out of Britain, Arthur would agree to stay out of Scotland. To everyone's surprise, Angus accepted Arthur's proposal. He even signed a peace treaty with Arthur. There was no telling how good his promises would be in the long run, but for now things had settled down quite nicely. Aside from the banished King Nentres, the only remaining thorn was the Danish mercenaries; and now, thanks to the good work of folks like Bedivere and Gwythir, the worst of the Danish groups had been dealt with.

As the evening wore on, I began to feel quite a bit better—my master was safe, the fighting in the north was practically over, and we would surely reach the friary tomorrow. Why, Arthur might even be there *now*. With that happy thought in mind, I curled myself up among the rushes on the floor of the great hall and was soon fast asleep.

Later that night I had a very vivid dream. I dreamed that Arthur had come to me right there in the great hall of Joyous Garde. I dreamed that he'd found his way to my little corner and that he'd plopped himself down beside me on the floor. My dream felt so real it hardly seemed like a dream at all; it was just as if Arthur had really come to me and touched me softly and whispered a gentle greeting in my ear.

In the wee hours of the dawning, as the first hints of morning crept through the hall's high windows, I raised my eyelids and looked around. The first thing I saw was Arthur! He was sound asleep, right beside me, with his knees pushed up against my back. My vivid dream hadn't been a dream at all. Arthur had come. *My master had come*

IV   You Can Run,
But You Can't Hide

The next morning everything was perfect. After we breakfasted on biscuits smothered in venison gravy, we set off for Crastor. It was the finest September morning you could possibly imagine. The sun was glinting off the gray-green sea and Nature was providing her grandest music— for waves were tumbling excitedly on the beach, and gulls and curlews were filling the air with their joyous, raucous cries.

Our trek along the coast from Joyous Garde to the village of Crastor was just right—far enough to get our juices flowing but not so far that we wished the journey any shorter. And when it was over, there stood Brother Blaise, watching for us. Things were truly perfect that morning, and I'll bet you know why. They were truly perfect because *Arthur* was there.

My goodness, we'd made it at last to St. Francis' Friary. It was a humble little place, really—just a small cluster of gray stone buildings huddled inside a dry stone wall. But it was in a very lovely spot, perched halfway up a hillside overlooking the sea and the village of Crastor. At last I would be meeting Brother Blaise, a fellow who was greatly loved by both Arthur and Merlin. And there he was, standing in front of the friary, shielding his eyes from the sun, watching as we approached. When he spotted us he started waving, and the young lad beside him began whooping and hollering. So this is it at last, I thought—journey's end.

Brother Blaise was a slender, stoop-shouldered old fellow with thin silver hair. He looked old, all right, though not quite so old as I'd expected. Don't forget, Brother Blaise was already a grown man when Merlin was born—and Merlin's not exactly a spring chicken. Yes, Brother Blaise was old all right; still, he had quite a ways to go before he'd be catching Methuselah.

"So this is Cabal," he said with a smile. Dropping to one knee, he placed his hands on the sides of my face and looked me in the eye. "Cabal, I'm eager to get to know you. I hope you'll be staying here long enough for me to do that. I certainly hope you and your master aren't planning to go rushing off again any time soon. I want the two of you to dump the cares of the world out here on the doorstep and have yourselves a truly restful visit."

"I would like that too, Brother Blaise," Arthur replied, "but I'm not so sure it will be possible. I should know more after our discussions tonight. But I have a feeling we may be going south again sooner than any of us would prefer."

"My word," said Brother Blaise still looking at me, "all this rushing about. All this talking and planning and fighting. Well, I'm sure it's important. But let's not have any of that for the next few hours, at least. Oh Arthur," he said, smiling from ear to ear, "it's so good to see you again! And it's so good to finally meet *you*, Cabal. I'll never forget how much your young master missed you when he and Kei were here before. I say, though, Arthur, you don't suppose Cabal would be ready for a bite of lunch, do you?"

"I'd say there's a pretty good chance of it," Arthur said with a grin. Lupus and I were soon sniffing and pawing at the meat pasties that Simon, Brother Blaise's young helper, had placed before us. They had a wild taste and weren't like anything we'd ever had. What was in them, we discovered, was hare meat, for the hillside behind the friary was teeming with those wild and crazy creatures.

And that's how Lupus and I spent our afternoon. While Arthur and Blaise sat on a bench in the sunshine and chatted away, Lupus and I rampaged about on the hillside, barking our fool heads off at those crazy critters who dashed all over in zig-zaggy patterns. I hope you won't think less of us for terrorizing those silly fellows; honestly, we didn't mean them any harm. We were just being our doggy selves. Besides, I think they enjoyed it as much as we did.

"You can run," I barked at them, "but you can't hide—do you hare me?"

As we were coming back, panting happily, our tongues hanging out, Simon came out to greet us. I felt a little sorry for the lad, for he walked with a limp and had a misshapen arm that he held close to his chest. But he was as good-natured as could be, and as he spoke to us and patted us, his eyes were bright and shiny.

"Been chasin' the wild hares, hey?" he said in his high-pitched voice. "Been stirrin' 'em up real good, hey? Been havin' yourselves a real fun time, hey?"

"Just keepin' those silly fellows on their toes," I barked back at him. "And keepin' ourselves in fighting trim. You never know when you'll need to be in fighting trim." Of course Simon couldn't understand me, but he was grinning like anything. My goodness, it felt so good to be there at the friary with Simon and Blaise and Arthur.

Later that day as the afternoon was waning, a group of riders appeared at the top of the hill behind the friary, their dark forms silhouetted against the sky. The way the light was shining it was hard to make out who they were. Then a voice boomed out over the hillside— "Lupus! Lupus!" Lupus went charging off for all he was worth, dashing up the hill toward his master Kei. I took off after him, nearly as eager to see Kei as he was.

Kei tumbled off Brutus, and then he and Lupus were rolling in the grass, wrestling and grabbing and hugging and licking. After they'd had their own special moment, I went charging in too, anxious to be in on the thing. "C'mere, you old grass-eater," Kei shouted at me. "C'mere and give me a proper welcome." I leaped up on Kei and gave him a big lick and then he gave me a big hug. All the while, Lupus was dancing and prancing around us.

"Hey, Kei!" came Arthur's voice from below, "supper's on the table. We don't plan to wait for any laggards!"

"Clear a space and pour the ale!" shouted Kei. "And if you rotters nab all the good stuff, may you roast in hell!"

After dinner, Arthur and Kei and the others remained around the refectory table where they'd dined, not quite ready to get down to the serious discussions they would soon be having. Simon scurried about, lugging away dishes and tidying things up. Brother Blaise, though, had disappeared, and I found myself wondering where he'd gone. I sniffed about and then tracked him down in his lair. He was in his own little room, bent over his worktable, scritch-scratching away. I didn't mean to be rude, but I was curious about what he was doing, so I brushed up against his leg.

"Well, Cabal," he said with a smile, "ferreted me out, have you? I thought I would just steal a few moments and jot down some of the things Arthur has been telling me. I wanted to get them down while they were fresh in my mind. My memory's not what it used to be." Then Blaise pointed at a huge leather-bound volume resting on the shelf above his head.

"Do you see that, Cabal? It's all about Merlin—about the events surrounding his birth and about a terrible tyrant named Vortigern who wanted to kill Merlin. Merlin was still just a very young boy—only six years old, he was—but my goodness, what a clever little lad. Merlin completely outsmarted that fellow, and *he* was the one who died, not Merlin. It's also about Uther Pendragon and how he came to be the High King of Britain. I've been writing these things down because they must never be forgotten. But the book I'm working on right now is only about Arthur. Let me see, now—I'm wondering if I've put anything in there about you, yet? Hmmm . . . no . . . I don't believe I have."

He hadn't put anything in there about *me*? I just cocked my head and stared. How could you tell the story of Arthur, I wondered, and not say anything about *me*?

"My goodness, Cabal, don't look so offended," said Brother Blaise. "I won't be leaving you out, I promise. I've a good bit more to do yet on this one, and you'll get all the credit you deserve. That's my solemn pledge."

Actually, I'd already begun to feel a little sheepish about my petty and selfish thoughts. On the other hand, though, it did seem to me that it would be a rather significant oversight if Brother Blaise's book didn't contain at least a *few* things about Arthur's loyal, loving, grass-eating companion—wouldn't you agree?

V   Good Friends
& Bad Tidings

Along about twilight that evening a great assemblage of folks had congregated in the friary's long, narrow refectory. Seated at the ancient wooden tables that ran the full length of the dining room were Arthur and Kei and Hervey; Sir Griflet, Sir Lucan, and Sir Bedivere; Cleodalis and Bertilak; Sir Tristrem, Sir Dagonet, and Gwythir the Pict. Brother Blaise, Brother John, and young Simon were there too, and last but not least, Emrys and Lupus and me. It seemed to me that all we needed now was for old Merlin to show up and then the whole gang would be there.

As darkness was falling a pair of riders appeared at the top of the same hill that Kei and Hervey had ridden over a few hours earlier. I looked out through the open door and studied them good, and it didn't take long to figure out who they were. One of them was Merlin, for the huge black horse he was riding could only be Bryn; the other rider, I was certain, was Nyneve.

Lupus and I charged out to greet them, but this time our cheerful barks and frolics were not warmly received. That, as we soon discovered, was because Merlin was in one of those dark moods he sometimes gets. Well, I could hardly blame him. He and Nyneve looked drawn and haggard. As it turned out, they'd been riding five straight days with hardly any rest or sleep. Even old Merlin has his limits, and for once he seemed to have reached them.

Knowing this wasn't a very good moment to be giving the old geezer a hard time, Lupus and I toned down our welcome by a couple of notches. When Nyneve climbed down from her horse, she stopped and patted us gently and smiled at us. But Merlin, with barely a glance at us, slid off of Bryn and shambled toward the friary, his hair and beard looking wilder than ever.

For a moment Merlin stood in the doorway, looking in and studying the great crowd that was gathered there. Warm greetings were shouted to him, but he didn't bother to acknowledge them. He just stood there staring. The room grew quiet while Merlin's tired old eyes moved slowly about, taking everyone in. When he spotted Gwythir, his eyes brightened for a moment, and the two of them exchanged nods.

At last Merlin said wearily, "You've done well, Arthur, very well indeed. And you, Kei, you've done *brilliantly*. But Arthur, I'm afraid I'm the bearer of bad news."

He stopped talking for a moment and reached out for the cup that Simon, who was standing there patiently, was holding for him. He drank a huge gulp and then smacked his lips. "My word, Blaise, that's what I call a noble brew. One of your best yet. Keep *that* up and in another fifty years you'll be Britain's finest brew master."

Merlin's wry remark brought a smile to Blaise's wrinkled old face, and I heard Dagonet's chuckles and Gwythir's high-pitched laughter. Despite Merlin's little joke, the atmosphere in the room remained tense. All those folks were on the edges of their seats, waiting to hear the ill tidings Merlin had come to deliver.

"It's the Saxons, isn't it," said Arthur, the only one there who dared prod Merlin when he was in one of his black moods.

"Of *course* it's the Saxons!" Merlin snapped back at him. "Yes, Arthur, it's the bloody Saxons, who right at this moment are swarming all over the south of Britain. They've taken the entire southeast. Now they're moving west."

"Even *London*?"

"No, London's survived—thanks to its massive walls and Bishop Baldwin's quick wits. But the city's completely cut off—a little British island in a Saxon sea. Yes, Arthur, it's the bloody Saxons all right! And their armies are *immense*."

"What about Lot?" Arthur asked. "The Saxons haven't defeated him, have they?"

"No, Lot's still all right. He's pulled back to Somerset. He's fortifying the old hillfort atop the Barren Down—as good a place as any to make a stand. But he's vastly outnumbered, Arthur—at least ten to one, maybe *twenty* to one! You've got to muster everyone you can and get them there. All the Britains must set aside their differences and rise up as one. We must fight the Saxons *now*. If we don't, it will be too late. The Saxons are reaching for our throats, Arthur, and they mean to *rip them out*!" I watched as Arthur's face tightened and the muscles in his neck stood out.

Young Simon tiptoed about the room, filling the cups and mugs of the somber folks who'd been drinking in Merlin's unwelcome words.

"All right, then," Arthur said grimly, "let's get down to it. Cleodalis, take twenty men and ride as swiftly as you can to Carmelide. Rally every able-bodied man there. *You'll* be the one in charge, Cleodalis, not Leodegrance. Tell him he must remain in Carmelide with Gwinevere—tell him those are *my orders*. And send messengers on to Uriens; if we're lucky, he already knows what's happening and is on his way to the Barren Down."

"Cleodalis," Merlin added, "make sure that Morgan accompanies Uriens to the Barren Down."

"Morgan le Fay, my lord?"

"Of *course* Morgan le Fay!" Merlin snapped. "Do you know any *other* Morgan? She's a better man than most of those we've got—and we may have need of her special talents. Never underestimate the value of an intelligent woman, Cleodalis!"

"No, my lord Merlin, I certainly won't."

Arthur made Tristrem responsible for organizing the army of the north, which would include the men from King Nentres' troop who'd sworn allegiance to Arthur. That would make quite a sizeable force once it was assembled, but it would take time to move it south. I wondered if they would be able to get there soon enough. Messengers were to be sent to King Mark in Cornwall, too, ordering him to bring the army of Cornwall north to the Barren Down.

"Lord Artos," said Gwythir, using a name for Arthur I'd never heard, "my people will wish to be there too. With your leave, I shall go and gather them now. Look for us at the Barren Down in five days' time." When Gwythir said that, eyebrows shot up all around the room.

"*Five days?*" said Kei. "With all due respect, my friend, that hardly seems possible."

"It is possible, my lord Kei. Do not think that it isn't."

After all the assignments had been made, everyone sat there quietly, talking softly and enjoying their final sips of Blaise's delicious nut-brown ale. They knew this would be their last quiet evening for some time to come.

Nyneve, I noticed, went over to Sir Lucan and whispered something in his ear. Then Sir Lucan began rummaging in his pack; what he brought out was a beautifully carved wooden box. He removed the lid and pulled out a magnificent object—it was the splendid cup that Gwinevere had given Arthur at Leodegrance's banquet. Arthur, observing what was going on, beckoned for Sir Lucan to bring him the cup.

"Before we go our separate ways," Arthur declared, holding the cup high above his head, "let us share in one last drink from the cup. Let us share a drink of courage and friendship and unity. Let us drink to what we have known before and what we shall hope to know again in days to come."

Simon filled the cup to the brim and carried it around the room, serving it to every person there. Before they drank, every person offered up a pledge or a prayer, some in loud bold voices and some so softly you could barely hear them.

"To victory," Sir Griflet said simply. He held the cup up as high as his arms could reach, holding it there for a moment. Then he brought the cup down to his lips and sipped.

"To the days of wine and roses," said Hervey, "may they never end."

"To King Lot and King Uriens and Morgan le Fay," said Bedivere, "may they survive and prosper until we arrive to aid them."

"To love and loyalty," said Sir Cleodalis, "to one's kith and kin."

"To the Land of Logres," said Sir Tristrem, "long may she endure."

"May the Lord's blessings be upon us all," said Brother John. He drank deeply from the cup and then crossed himself.

"To the never-ending cycle of all things," said Gwythir, with his face lifted and his eyes shut tight. He held the cup up to his nose and breathed in its aroma but he didn't drink from it.

"To Arthur and Kei, to Brother Blaise and Merlin, to Nyneve and Jennie, to Cabal and Lupus," said Emrys. He spoke so softly it took the very keen ears of a very keen dog to hear what he was saying. He handed the cup to Simon and then reached inside his tunic for the pouch that held his amulet; of course his amulet wasn't there for he'd given it to Jennie. Maybe something else was there? Maybe something Jennie had given to Emrys?

"To the earth, the moon, the sun, and the stars," mumbled Merlin, and when he drank, he accidentally sloshed his beard with ale. Way to go, Merlin, I laughed to myself, you clumsy old goat! Merlin glared at me for a moment out of the corner of his eye; and then he shot me a wink.

When Simon handed the cup to Nyneve, her words were so soft I'm probably the only one who heard them. "To caring and kindness," she whispered.

When it was Arthur's turn he repeated what he said earlier. "To courage and friendship and unity."

Brother Blaise was the last to drink. Simon handed the cup to him carefully, and Blaise nodded his thanks. With lowered head he whispered, "Thy will be done."

Towards the end of the evening some of the folks were preparing to depart. One of them was Gwythir, who would be riding north to collect as many of his friends as he could. Dagonet, who had become Gwythir's very close friend, went over to say his farewells. Gwythir grinned at Dagonet and gave him a hug. Dagonet said he would see him again in a week or two at the Barren Down.

"Indeed you will, Sir minstrel-knight, indeed you will. But I have an important request for you, Sir minstrel-knight. I very much hope that by the time you get to the Barren Down you will have prepared some new songs. My companions, you should know, will require much amusing."

"What kind of songs will they want to hear, Gwythir?"

"The ones you are best at, of course—those very *silly* songs."

"What!" said Dagonet, sounding deeply offended. "You mean they won't want to hear my tender love songs or my bold ballads of derring-do?"

"No, my friend, indeed they will not," said Gwythir, just barely cracking a smile.

VI   Be Swift to Love,
Make Haste to be Kind

Since it was going to be both our *first* and our *last* night at the friary—this place we'd been trying to get to for a month of Sundays—I decided to curl up and sleep on the floor next to the little bunk of Brother Blaise. He was a kindly old fellow and I understood why Arthur and Merlin loved him so much. I wanted to share a little closeness with him because I suspected it would be quite a while before we would see him again. I think he was pleased that I did. He nestled an old blanket around me and patted my head tenderly. "You're quite a fellow, Cabal," he said softly. "Arthur is lucky to have such a friend."

After I'd been asleep for a bit I was awaked by the sound of footsteps. Someone was moving down the hallway in the direction of the kitchen. Curious about this, I slipped out of my little nest and went to take a look. Someone, it seemed to me, was trying very hard not to make a sound. Then I saw that that someone was Simon, Brother Blaise's young helper. I spied on him as he crept softly into the kitchen. He was clutching something tightly against his chest—my word, it was the beautiful cup Gwinevere had given to Arthur, the beautiful cup everyone had been drinking from earlier in the evening!

Simon reached into a cupboard and brought out a pitcher. Slowly and carefully he poured a good part of its contents into the cup, and then he picked it up and moved cautiously toward the friary door. What in the world was he up to? I doubted if he was trying to *steal* the cup. That wasn't the kind of person he was. Yet judging by his furtive behavior, he knew full well that he wasn't supposed to be handling the cup. He must've nabbed it out of Sir Lucan's pack after Sir Lucan had fallen asleep.

As I listened, I heard Simon settling down on the bench just outside the friary door. When I stuck my nose outside to have a look, the poor lad nearly jumped out of his skin. "Oh, Cabal," he whispered, sounding relieved, "it's *you*! Keepin' an eye on me, hey? Can't fool those sharp little ears of yours, hey? Well, c'mon out here, then. C'mon and be joinin' me."

I climbed up onto the bench and snuggled up against Simon. That's when I discovered what he'd poured into the cup. It was milk. Simon looked at me out of the corner of his eye, and then he lifted the cup to his lips. "Here's to you, Cabal," he said. "And here's to Father Blaise, hey? He's my spiritual father, Cabal. He's the closest thing I've ever had to a *real* father. I love him, Cabal. He's the kindest person I've ever known."

Then Simon did a wonderful thing. He placed the cup down beside the bench and motioned with his head. He was telling me it was *my* turn to take a drink. He was telling me that he wanted me to join him in drinking from the cup. Well, *why not*?

I sniffed at the fresh milk and then I lapped some of it up. Yumm, tasty. Just for good measure, I lapped up a little more.

There I was, sitting outside the old friary, sitting beside a lad named Simon, looking out at that dark night, lapping up some lovely fresh milk from Gwinevere's beautiful cup—now, who would *ever* have predicted *that*?

Then I understood what Simon was doing. What he was doing was no different from what all the others had been doing a just few hours earlier. They'd been drinking from the cup and making their pledge or saying their prayer. Now it was Simon's turn. Simon wasn't a knight and he wasn't a member of Arthur's troop and he wouldn't be going off to do battle at the Barren Down. He was just an ordinary and unimportant young serving lad who'd been taken in at the friary through the kindness of Brother Blaise. But it seemed to me that Simon was just as entitled to make his pledge or say his prayer as anyone else. He needed to pledge his love to Brother Blaise, the one person in the world who meant everything to him.

To Simon, Brother Blaise was the one who really mattered. And that got me thinking. All of the folks gathered at the friary were people I really cared about, and I hoped and prayed that nothing bad was going to happen to any of them in the difficult days ahead. But as much as I cared about all those folks, there were a special few who mattered most of all. I'd only known him for a short time, but Brother Blaise was one of them; he was a very special person. But it was Arthur and Merlin who mattered to me most of all. Arthur and Merlin were my two best friends in the world.

The ones that really mattered, I thought. For each of us there are just a few of them, very special folks who mean the world to us. To Simon, it was Brother Blaise. To Jennie, it was Emrys. To Bertilak, it was Cleodalis. To Merlin, it was Arthur and Nyneve. To Arthur, it was Kei and Merlin and Gwinevere and me.

Yes, *me*. To Arthur, I was one of the ones who really mattered. And to me it was Arthur. Arthur—the kindest, gentlest, lovingest master any dog has ever had.

AUTHOR'S NOTE

In *A CUP OF KINDNESS* the fledgling king is attempting to establish order in a realm filled with petty rivalries and personal grievances amongst the lesser kings and nobles. Some of Britain's lesser kings, such as King Ryence of Northgales, have refused to accept Arthur as King Uther Pendragon's rightful heir. Others are supporting the new king with great reluctance or are only pretending to support the king. Arthur's first responsibility is to establish order within the land and to put down the rebels. But just as he is achieving this goal, the external threats to Britain, which King Uther had so greatly feared, have become more magnified than ever. As the novel ends, the Britons realize they are facing a life and death struggle for the continued existence of a nation.

*   *   *   *

Songs & Poems. Jennie's song on pp. 115-16 was adapted from an old, anonymous English ballad. Brother John's song on pp. 131-32 is a very free paraphrase of Psalm 19 from the Old Testament *Book of Psalms*. Taliesin's Christmas song on p. 124 of *THE DRAGON STONE* is based upon a Middle English lyric poem. All of the other poems and songs in both *THE DRAGON STONE* and *A CUP OF KINDNESS* can be safely attributed to the canine author.

*   *   *   *

Images & Illustrations. Nearly all of the images and illustrations used in both *THE DRAGON STONE* and *A CUP OF KINDNESS* were inspired by medieval sources. Several of them have been adapted from the author's photographs of medieval castles or churches; the image on p. 14, for example, comes from a photo taken at Modena Cathedral in Italy; the doorway on p. 134 is from the author's photo of Penmon Priory in Angelsey, Wales. Others are loosely based upon manuscript illustrations or illuminations, carvings in stone or wood, wood block illustrations, or the like. Only a few of them are original drawings.

*   *   *   *

If you enjoyed *A CUP OF KINDNESS*,
would you be willing to order a copy for a friend?

☐ Yes, here's my check for $14.50 which includes shipping.
Please send a copy to:

Name: _____

Address: _____
_____ Zip: _____

☐ Please put me on the mailing list for future titles in this
series.

Name: _____

Address: _____

_____

Please send checks to:
Pale Horse Productions
108 Maid Marion Place
Williamsburg, VA 23185